凱信企管

用對的方法充實自己，
讓人生變得更美好！

凱信企管

用對的方法充實自己，
讓人生變得更美好！

USER'S GUIDE
使用說明

英語聊天，不再當句點王！

不論是運動、美食、購物、穿搭……想怎麼聊都可以！
帶你破冰、不尬聊，自信、流暢地用英語順利開啟話匣子，
閒聊生活樂事！

第 8 章 哈啦下廚
角色：哈哈（來自台灣）、Lyla（來自美國）
I'll cook.
You wanna get something to eat?
Is there a problem?
......
You can complain in the morning.
You're a horrible cook.

1 輕鬆趣味的漫畫小劇場導入話題，學習更生動

以有趣的漫畫方式，精準勾勒主題情境；學習破冰技巧，啟動聊天話題。

2 25 項生活主題 X 250 個聊天情境 X 750 句擴充句，輕鬆聊不停

全書超過 1000 句的哈啦會話，吃喝玩樂主題明確，讓你橫向 → 不斷開展話題，縱向 → 持續深入內容；交朋友、生活互動，無冷場、聊天不卡關， 一來一往超流暢。

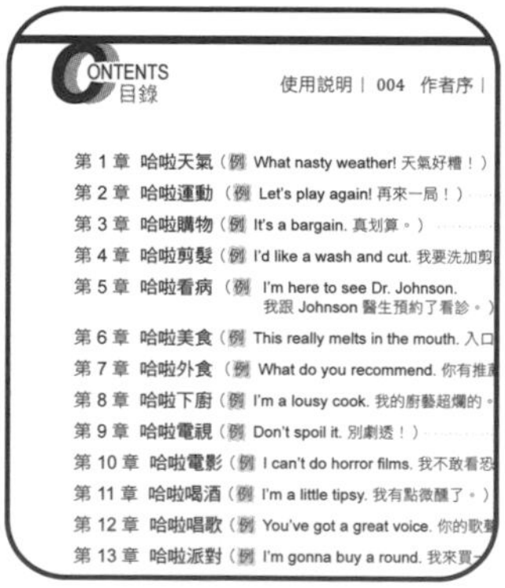

CONTENTS 目錄
使用說明 | 004 作者序 |
第 1 章 哈啦天氣（例 What nasty weather! 天氣好糟！）
第 2 章 哈啦運動（例 Let's play again! 再來一局！）
第 3 章 哈啦購物（例 It's a bargain. 真划算。）
第 4 章 哈啦剪髮（例 I'd like a wash and cut. 我要洗加剪
第 5 章 哈啦看病（例 I'm here to see Dr. Johnson. 我跟 Johnson 醫生預約了看診。）
第 6 章 哈啦美食（例 This really melts in the mouth. 入口
第 7 章 哈啦外食（例 What do you recommend. 你有推
第 8 章 哈啦下廚（例 I'm a lousy cook. 我的廚藝超爛的。
第 9 章 哈啦電視（例 Don't spoil it. 別劇透！）
第 10 章 哈啦電影（例 I can't do horror films. 我不敢看恐
第 11 章 哈啦喝酒（例 I'm a little tipsy. 我有點微醺了。）
第 12 章 哈啦唱歌（例 You've got a great voice. 你的歌
第 13 章 哈啦派對（例 I'm gonna buy a round. 我來買

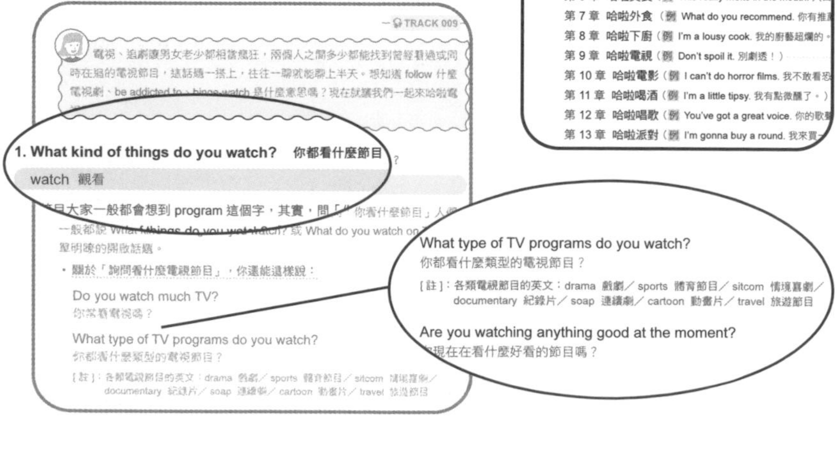

TRACK 009
1. What kind of things do you watch? 你都看什麼節目
watch 觀看
關於「詢問看什麼電視節目」，你還能這樣說：
Do you watch much TV?
你常看電視嗎？
What type of TV programs do you watch?
你都看什麼類型的電視節目？
[註]：各類電視節目的英文：drama 戲劇／ sports 體育節目／ sitcom 情境喜劇／ documentary 紀錄片／ soap 連續劇／ cartoon 動畫片／ travel 旅遊節目
Are you watching anything good at the moment?
你現在在看什麼好看的節目嗎？

③ 必學關鍵字＋重要詞彙＋慣用語，英語口說一次達陣

- ▲ 拉出每一情境的重要單字或較難詞彙，有效擴增單詞量，快速抓住聽／說重點。
- ▲ 老外常用慣用語以對話的方式設計，輕鬆理解相關的英語進階使用方式，提升英語力！

跟八卦有關的慣用語

1. juicy gossip　有料的八卦

哈哈：What do you do on your girls' night out?
你們姊妹淘之夜都在做什麼？

Lyla：Talking about all that juicy gossip! That's what we do decompress.
當然是聊八卦啊！那是我們解壓的方式。

8. He's a player.　他是個花心男。

player　玩咖

關於各種渣男壞女的情慧想必大
障礙，心都渡變的一起，
……最。我想這壓談就是聊八卦之所以
吧！

- 關於「八卦渣男渣女」，你還能這樣說：
So she cheated on him?

cheat 欺騙	two-timing 劈腿的
surprise 使驚訝	flirtatious 輕挑的

④ 學習 Plus，一魚多吃，延伸學更多

- ▲「你還能這樣說」，說英文更靈活
  EX：I'm just browsing.
  （我只是隨便看看。）
  換個說法：I'm just looking.

- ▲ 異國文化特色、資訊分享
  分享更多與主題／情境相關的資訊，也提醒不同文化及生活習慣上的差異，幫助你與他人互動過程中，不犯人、不踩雷。

- ▲ 外師 mp3 音檔
  外師親錄語音檔，250 個聊天主題 750 句擴充句全都錄。隨掃即聽，時時都能練習道地口語及敏銳聽力。

9. It's a bargain.　真划算。

bargain　便宜的價格

中文講的「殺價」，英文可不是 killing the price 喔！
bargain 作為名詞時，原指「便宜貨」，也能引伸為「
次當你買到物美價廉的東西時，發自內心的來一句：It's

- 關於「划算」，你還能這樣說：
  It's a steal.
  真划算。

— 🎧 TRACK 003 —

1. Exc
Q-tip

……這……Excuse me.
……………… I'm looking for... ……
安。

- 關於「詢問賣的東西」，你還能這樣說：
  Excuse me. Do you have washing-up bowls?

  Excuse me. Where can I find duvet covers?

  Excuse me. I wonder if you've got vacuum cleaners?

全書音檔雲端連結

因各家手機系統不同，若無法直接掃描，仍可以至（https://tinyurl.com/25nx6278）電腦結雲端下載！

PREFACE
前言

　　我有很多學生背了很多單字和文法規則，但面對外國人開口時，卻出現一口尷尬的啞巴英語。這些學生，不是他們不夠努力，而是施力點不正確。就像學鋼琴只學樂理，不上琴彈奏一樣。

　　既然我們的目的是溝通，何不將問題簡單化，直接學溝通所需的句子呢？大家想想，平常我們講話時，多半都是以「句子」為單位的，但在英文課上，老師一般都要求我們背「單字」、分析「文法」，再將成串的單字根據文法規則排列組合成我們要的句子。結構簡單的句子還好，如果是多個子句組成的複雜句，豈不想半天？

　　如果我們繞過複雜的文法，直接學習實用的句子，不是直接能完成溝通任務嗎？當我們養成背句子的習慣，我們可以省掉繁複的思考工序，直接根據語境以句子來回應，這樣反倒是更相似於母語習得過程的。再者，在具備溝通能力的基礎上去學文法，對語言的認知會更全面，對語言的運用還能達到加乘的效果。

　　這本書根據 25 個話題整理出了口語對話中常用的 1000 個英文句子，包含了人生中常遇到的各種聊天話題。在這裡我們不談太多的文法，不過度分析語言，我們不只記單字，還直接記句子。只要將這本書慢慢消化吸收後，相信下次和老外聊天時，你會發現你的口語變得更溜了喔！

CONTENTS 目錄

使用説明 | 004　作者序 | 006

第1章 哈啦天氣

角色：哈哈（來自台灣）、Lyla（來自美國）

天氣雖然是個很好的破冰話題，但如果你也像哈哈這樣只會 so hot、very hot、really hot 的話，那不僅會顯得非常單調，而且很快就會讓話題句點囉！想要聊天氣也能聊得很高招、很道地，我們就來學學以下十句話，一起哈啦天氣吧！

1. What's the weather like out there?　今天天氣怎麼樣？

> What's ... like?　……如何？／ out there　外面

問「今天天氣如何？」What's the weather like out there? 是最簡單、最普遍的問法。或者，我們也可以問 How's the weather out there?

- 關於「問天氣」，你還能這樣說：

What is it like out there?
現在天氣怎麼樣？

What's the forecast for today?
今天天氣預報怎麼樣？

What's the weather going to be like today?
今天整天的天氣如何？

> **forecast** 預報

2. It's a lovely day, isn't it?　今天天氣真好。

> lovely　美好的

lovely 這個字可以用來形容人，表示「可愛的」、「迷人的」、「美麗的」，同時也能用來形容某事物是「令人愉悅的」。所以，下次如果你要表達「今天天氣真好」時，不要再只會說 The weather is nice. 囉！

- 關於「天氣好」，你還能這樣說：

It's a beautiful day.
今天天氣真好。

It's warm and sunny today.
今天晴朗溫暖。

We couldn't ask for nicer weather.
天氣好到不能再好了。

3. What nasty weather! 天氣好糟！

nasty 惡劣的

nasty 是個語氣很強烈的，表示「令人厭惡的」形容詞。用來形容「糟到讓人絕望的天氣」相當適合。搭配感嘆句 What a ...! 是不是很能抒發被壞天氣抑鬱著的心情呢？

• 關於「壞天氣」，你還能這樣說：

Awful weather today, isn't it?
今天天氣真差，不是嗎？

What gloomy weather we're having!
今天天氣真令人憂鬱！

I've had enough of this weather.
我受夠這天氣了。

awful 糟的	gloomy 陰鬱的	have enough of 受夠了……

4. It's a scorcher outside. 外面超熱的。

scorcher 大熱天

scorch 的意思是「燒焦」、「烤焦」，而 scorcher 則是指「非常炙熱的東西」，在談論天氣的語境中可引申為「大熱天」。當天氣熱到讓人受不了時，就可以用這個句子。

• 關於「熱」，你還能這樣說：

It's burning hot / blazing hot / sweltering / sultry outside.
外面天氣超熱。
[註]：sweltering 和 sultry 特別是形容「炎熱潮濕的天氣」。

I'm sweating like a pig / bullets.
我現在汗流浹背。

I'm melting now.
我快融化了。

blazing 炎熱的	sweltering 悶熱的	sultry 悶熱的
sweat 流汗；汗	bullet 子彈	melt 融化

5. I'm frozen to the bone.　我快凍死了。

frozen 凍僵的／ bone 骨頭

frozen 的意思是「被凍僵的」，而 frozen to the bone 就是指「凍到骨頭裡了」。描述冷到刺骨的低溫，這個句子再精準不過了。

• 關於「冷」，你還能這樣說：

It's freezing / chilly / frigid / biting cold outside.
外面天氣好冷。

You have to bundle / wrap up before going outside.
你出門前必須多穿衣服喔。

I just want to snuggle in my bed.
我只想要窩在床裡。

freezing 冷凍的	chilly 寒冷的	frigid 寒冷的
bundle up 穿得暖和	wrap up 穿得暖和	snuggle 依偎

6. It looks like it's going to rain.　好像快下雨了。

it looks like... 好像；似乎

當天空陰沉沉的，空氣中散發著雨的氣味，好像再過不久就要下雨了，我們就可以用上這句話，提醒大家出門記得帶雨具喔！有時候，我們想要懶惰一點時，也可以只說 Looks like rain.。

- 關於「下雨」，你還能這樣說：

It's drizzling / pouring outside.

下毛毛雨／大雨了。

It's really coming down out there.

外面下大雨了。

The rain is not going to let up anytime soon.

這雨短時間之內不會停的。

drizzle 下毛毛雨	pour 傾倒	let up 停歇

7. It's been snowing for two days. 已經下了兩天雪了。

snow 下雪

下雪對居住在溫暖地區的人來說往往是新奇而令人興奮的，但在多雪的地區，持續不停的降雪，不僅容易帶來許多不便，也會讓人心情沉重、視覺疲乏。這時候，如果要表達「已經下了多久的雪了」，我們可以用「現在完成進行式」It's been snowing for ... 的這個句子。

- 關於「下雪」，你還能這樣說：

It's snowing!

下雪了！

I'm going to make a snowman.

我要堆雪人。

[註]：注意！不是 do a snowman，是 make a snowman 喔！

It's going to stop in an hour or two.

下過一兩個小時雪就會停了。

snowman 雪人

8. I'm getting used to the strange weather. 我快習慣這種怪天氣了。

> get used to 習慣／strange 奇怪的

冬天的颱風、夏天的熱浪，甚至是天空下起了青蛙和魚……層出不窮的各種天氣異象，讓我們人類不禁感嘆：地球真的壞掉了！而怪奇的天氣現象也成了現代人話家常的主題呢！談論異常天氣時，說說這句話來表達你的無奈！

- 關於「怪天氣」，你還能這樣說：

The wind was blowing like crazy.
這風颳得簡直太可怕了。

The heat is unbearable. Is it really winter?
這高溫簡直太難受了。現在真的是冬天嗎？

What's going on with the weather?
天氣到底怎麼了？

heat 溫度	unbearable 無法忍受的

9. The forecast calls for blue skies on the weekend.
天氣預報說週末都是大晴天。

> forecast 預報／call for 預測

週末跟朋友計畫好要外出玩耍了，查看一下天氣預報，告知你的朋友週末的天氣如何，不妨使用 the forecast calls for ... 試試喔！

- 關於「天氣預報」，你還能這樣說：

There's a blizzard coming our way.
有一場暴風雪要來了。

We're expecting a spell of heavy rain this afternoon.
今天下午會下一陣大雨。

We're in for nasty weather for the rest of the week.
這週接下來幾天的天氣都很差。

blizzard 暴風雪	spell 一段時間	nasty 惡劣的
rest 剩下的部分		

10. It is always raining in Seattle.　西雅圖老是下雨。

Seattle　西雅圖

如果要跟朋友介紹一個城市大致的天氣狀況，我們可以用 It is always V-ing ... 的句型。又比如：「北京的冬天老是下雪。」我們可以說：It is always snowing in Beijing in winter.

- 關於「某地氣候的介紹」，你還能這樣說：

It gets extremely cold here in the wintertime.
這裡的冬天超級冷。

You may get flash floods here in the summer.
這裡的夏天可能會淹水。

It is one of the sunniest cities in all of America.
它是全美國最晴朗的城市之一。

extremely 極度地	flash flood 暴洪水

 跟天氣有關的慣用語

1. rain or shine　無論晴雨，一定到。

哈哈：Are you coming to my party tomorrow?
　　　妳明天要來參加我的派對嗎？

Lyla：Rain or shine.
　　　無論晴雨，一定到！

2. to take a raincheck   用於拒絕邀約

哈哈：Do you want to play some tennis tonight?
今天晚上要打網球嗎？

Lyla：I will take a raincheck on that.
先不了吧！

3. under the weather   身體微恙

哈哈：Are you OK? You don't look well.
妳還好嗎？妳臉色不太好。

Lyla：I am feeling a bit under the weather.
我有點不舒服。

4. It never rains but it pours.   屋漏偏逢連夜雨

哈哈：I don't know what's with me. I lost my wallet last week,

dropped my phone and broke it yesterday, and today I got

into a car accident.
我不知道怎麼回事。上禮拜我丟了皮夾，昨天摔碎了手機，然後今天又發生了車禍。

Lyla：Well, it never rains but it pours.
嗯……真是屋漏偏逢連夜雨。

5. rainbow chase   做白日夢

Lyla：I hope I can marry a billionaire someday.
我希望有一天可以嫁給一個億萬富翁。

哈哈：Stop your rainbow chase.
別做白日夢了。

第 2 章 哈啦運動

角色：哈哈（來自台灣）、Lyla（來自美國）

運動最容易讓人打開話匣子了！因此，在運動場上，我們除了交流球技外，語言的交流有時更是精彩！所以，想要一邊運動、一邊學習如何用英語交際嗎？那就千萬別像 Lyla 一樣，聽到要運動時就藉口百出喔！

1. Let's play some basketball.　一起去打籃球吧！

basketball 籃球

跟三五好友一起相約運動最紓壓了！這句 Let's play some... 可以用在任何的球類運動，意思是「一起去打一下……」。

• 關於「相約運動」，你還能這樣說：

It's Friday! Football time!
星期五！足球時間囉！

Let's go hit the gym.
一起去健身房吧！

Do you want to work out?
要去健個身嗎？

soccer 足球	hit the gym 上健身房	work out 健身

2. I want to lose a bit of weight.　我想減重。

lose weight 減重

走進健身房前立下各種目標，開始健身時驚覺自己想像力過於豐富，走出健身房後才發現，宵夜才是自己唯一的救贖。這種情景是否似曾相識呢？嘴上說說大家都會，但實際操作後才發現最不缺的永遠是藉口。但，說總是要說的啊！（壞笑）

• 關於「相約運動」，你還能這樣說：

I want to get a six-pack.
我想練六塊肌。

I want to trim down a bit.
我想要自己瘦一點點。

I want to bulk up.
我想練得壯一點。

| six-pack 六塊腹肌 | trim down 瘦身 | bulk up 變得壯實 |

3. I'm doing 100 push-ups in a row.　我要連做一百個伏地挺身。

push-up 伏地挺身／in a row 連續

do 是一個萬用動詞，後面可以接各種鍛鍊項目，比如：do push-ups 做伏地挺身、do sit-ups 做仰臥起坐、do some warm-ups 做點暖身、do some stretches 做點伸展、do a handstand 倒立。

• 關於「鍛鍊項目」，你還能這樣說：

Let's start with the warm-up.
一開始先來暖身。

Let's stretch before we start running.
跑步前先來伸展一下。

I'm gonna run 5 laps within 10 minutes.
我要在十分鐘內跑完五圈。

| warm up 暖身 | stretch 伸展 | lap 圈 |
| within 在……範圍內 | | |

4. I'm gonna crush you.　我要打垮你！

crush 擊垮

比賽前向對手撂狠話，給自己助助威、漲漲氣勢，順便練練嘴皮子，不正是跟運動夥伴打球時常做的事嗎？其中，我們常說的「電爆你」的英文就是用 crush 這個動詞，用起來比 beat 更有力道呢！

- 關於「向對手放狠話」，你還能這樣說：

I'll show you who's the boss.
我會讓你看看誰才是老大。

I'll give it my best shot.
我會展現我的十成功力。

I'm in great shape today.
我今天狀態超好！

| give it my best shot 盡全力 | in great shape 狀態極好 |

5. I'm on fire! 我發威了！

on fire 狀態超級好

競技賽場上，最迷人的風景是揮汗如雨的運動員，而最悅耳的聲音就是場上此起彼伏的加油聲了！不管是選手打了一個好球之後為自己激勵，還是場下的啦啦隊向場上運動員的喊話助威，都讓人熱血沸騰、青春感爆棚！有時候，場上的加油聲，不僅熱血，還很幽默！例如：要誇自己狀態超好，我們可以説：I'm on fire!「我著火啦！」

- 關於「比賽時的激勵語言」，你還能這樣說：

Go! Go! Go!
加油！加油！加油！

Way to go!
幹得漂亮！

Come on! Come on!
加油！加油！

| come on 加油 |

6. That was definitely the point of the match.

剛剛那球一定是本場最佳好球！

> definitely 必定／ point 分／ match 比賽

有沒有打球時遇到自己處於神級狀態的時候呢？或是對手好球不斷，自己在甘拜下風之餘，也忍不住要誇上幾句？展現自己的風度，也展現自己的英語，在出現好球時，來一句 That was definitely the point of the match! 誇誇對手吧！其中，the point of the match 就是「本場最佳好球」的意思。其他相似的結構還有 the time of my life，意思是「人生中最快樂的時光」。

• 關於「稱讚對手的激勵語言」，你還能這樣說：

That was an incredible point.
真是不可思議的一球！

Unbelievable shot!
不可思議的一球！

What a recovery!
救得真漂亮！

incredible 不可思議的	unbelievable 令人不敢相信的	recovery 恢復

7. I'm getting back into shape.　我狀態慢慢恢復了。

> get back into shape 恢復狀態

球場上有時球技不如人，但氣勢不能輸人啊！當自己狀態處於谷底時，對自己信心喊話：I'm getting back into shape. 不僅激勵自己，也順勢嚇嚇對手，讓對方不要太囂張喔！

• 關於「恢復狀態」，你還能這樣說：

I'm bouncing back.
我要反攻了！

I'm back in the game.
我狀態恢復囉！

I'm coming back!
我要反擊了！

bounce 反彈

8. You took me easily.　你贏我贏得太輕鬆了。

take 拿下

比賽完後，如果自己輸了，也別讓天被聊死啊！有風度的承認自己技不如人，是一個很容易開展新話題的方法。這句 You took me easily. 意思便是「你輕取了我」。對方多半都會回說：I was just lucky.「我只是比較幸運啦！」這時，我們就能繼續問：When did you start playing?「你什麼時候開始打球的？」或相關的問題，讓話題能持續延伸下去。

• 關於「甘拜下風」，你還能這樣說：

That was a landslide victory.
簡直是一面倒。

It was a one-sided match.
真是場一面倒的比賽。

You are better. No doubt about it.
還是你厲害！我沒話說！

landslide victory 壓倒性勝利	one-sided 單方面的	doubt 質疑

9. I'm done. 我不行了。

> done 結束了的

運動到累癱時，如果只會說 I'm so tired.，那根本不足以表達精疲力盡的感覺。如果要表達「我不行了」，英文我們可以說 I'm done.。done 的意思是「完成了的」、「結束了的」，在這個語境中有「體力消耗殆盡了」或「我不想再打了」的意思。

• 關於「體力耗盡」，你還能這樣說：

That's enough for me.
我體力不行了。

That's too much for me.
我負荷不了了。

I can't catch my breath.
我喘不過氣了。

| **enough** 足夠的 | **catch one's breath** 喘口氣 |

10. Let's play again! 再來一局！

> play 打球

這句話可以用在輸了不服氣，想再來一局翻盤，或是打完球後意猶未盡，和球友相約下次再戰的情境。在其他情況下，我們也可以說：Let's do this again! 或是 We should totally do this again! 來表達這次玩得很開心，下次再約的心情。

• 關於「相約再運動」，你還能這樣說：

I want a rematch.
我想要再來一局。

We should play again some time.
我們以後再來打！

This was fun! We should do this more often.

真好玩！我們應該常常來打！

---

rematch　重賽

 ## 跟運動有關的慣用語

1. The ball is in your court.　這是你自己要做的決定。

哈哈：Do you think I should quit my job?

　　　妳覺得我要辭職嗎？

Lyla：I don't know. The ball is in your court.

　　　我不知道，這是你自己要做的決定。

2. Monday morning quarterback　放馬後砲的人

哈哈：I knew the party wasn't fun. You shouldn't have gone!

　　　我就知道那派對一定不好玩，你真不應該去的！

Lyla：Shut up! Monday morning quarterback.

　　　閉嘴！馬後砲！

3. front runner　領先的人；贏面大的人

哈哈：Who do you think is going to be the next director?

　　　妳覺得誰會是下一任的主管呢？

Lyla：I think Joe is a front runner for the position.

　　　我覺得 Joe 接任主管的機率很大。

4. get the ball rolling　開始做某事

哈哈：I am thinking about advertising my studio flat sometime.

　　　我想之後來登我的套房公寓的廣告。

Lyla：Don't just think. Let's get the ball rolling by posting an
ad on Facebook.

　　　別光想，現在就去做，在臉書上登廣告吧！

5. keep your eye on the ball　集中精力

哈哈：I don't think I'm ready for this.

我覺得我還沒準備好。

Lyla：Come on! This is an important stage of your life. You need to keep your eye on the ball.

喂！現在是你人生的關鍵階段，你必須集中精力！

第３章　哈啦購物

角色：哈哈（來自台灣）、Lyla（來自美國）

購物總是讓人腎上腺素大爆發！不管是聖誕季的大減價，或是買到 CP 值爆表的戰利品，都讓人按耐不住心中的雀躍，想要立馬與朋友分享，好康逗相報！又或者在國外瘋狂血拚時，卻常常因為卡卡的英文而戰力受挫嗎？來學學哈啦購物的十大金句，一起暢快血拚吧！

1. Excuse me. I'm looking for Q-tips.　不好意思。我在找棉花棒。

Q-tip　棉花棒

找不到想買的東西向店員詢問時，一定要禮貌地用 Excuse me. 來開頭喔！而找東西最常用的句子就是 I'm looking for...。這絕對是出國購物必備金句了。用起來！

• 關於「詢問要買的東西」，你還能這樣說：

Excuse me. Do you have washing-up bowls?
不好意思。請問你們有賣洗碟盆嗎？

Excuse me. Where can I find duvet covers?
不好意思。請問被套在哪裡？

Excuse me. I wonder if you've got vacuum cleaners?
不好意思。請問你們有賣吸塵器嗎？

washing-up bowl 洗碟盆	duvet cover　被套	wonder　想知道
vacuum cleaner　吸塵器		

2. I'm fine, just browsing.　沒關係，我就看看而已。

browse　瀏覽

有時候我們逛街只是想隨興看看，並沒有特意想買什麼。這時當店員過來詢問你：Are you looking for something in particular? 時，我們就可以說 I'm fine, just

browsing. 來禮貌地表示自己只是想隨便看看，不需要店員的協助。如果直接説：
No! 當然也可以，但是是相當不禮貌的喔。

• 關於「婉拒店員服務」，你還能這樣說：

I'm OK. I'm just looking.
沒關係，我只是隨便看看。

It's OK, thanks. I'm just looking around.
沒關係，謝謝！我只是隨便看看。

I'm just seeing if there is anything I need.
我只是看看有沒有我需要的東西。

look around 四處看看

3. Can I get a discount on this?　這個有特價嗎？

discount 折扣

不管聖誕季大減價、換季大拍賣還是不定期的清倉出售，低價總是讓人流口水。
不管什麼時候，下手之前別忘了先問問：Can I get a discount on this?（笑）

• 關於「詢問特價」，你還能這樣說：

Can you give me a better deal?
你可以算我便宜一點嗎？

What's the price after the discount?
折扣後多少錢？

Are you having a sale?
你們有做特價嗎？

deal 交易	discount 折扣	sale 特價

4. Do you have this in another color? 這個有別的顏色的嗎？

當我們看中一樣產品，卻想要不同的顏色或尺寸時，我們可以問：Do you have this in another color? 或 Do you have this in another size? 如果想要 2XL 的尺碼，我們可以說：Do you have this in 2XL? 如果想要藍色的，我們可以說：Do you have this in blue? 以此類推。這邊的 in 後面接的是產品的「款式」。

• 關於「詢問產品款式」，你還能這樣說：

What is this made of?
這是什麼材質的？

[註]：衣物材質的英文：

cotton 棉／ silk 絲／ wool 羊毛／ linen 亞麻／ nylon 尼龍／ plastic 塑膠／ acrylic 壓克力紗／ leather 皮／ denim 牛仔布／ polyester 聚酯纖維

Do you have anything smaller?
你們有小一點的嗎？

Are these all you've got?
你們就只有這些嗎？

be made of 由……製成

5. Does it come with a guarantee? 這個有附保固嗎？

come with 附帶／ guarantee 保固書

guarantee「保固」、「保修」就是指產品在保固期內出現問題或發現瑕疵，公司或代理商所提供的售後服務和維修保障。買家在購買商品時最好了解清楚保固條款和細項，以免自己權益受損喔！在本句當中，come with 是一個很形象、很好用的片語，意思是「附帶」。

• 關於「詢問商品售後服務」，你還能這樣說：

Is this fully refundable?
這個可以全額退款嗎？

Who do I speak to about making a complaint?

請問我能向誰申請客訴？

Is this still under warranty?

這個還有保固嗎？

fully 全部	refundable 可退款的	complaint 投訴
warranty 保修		

6. Do you take credit cards?　我可以刷信用卡嗎？

> take 接受／ credit card 信用卡

在歐、美洲刷卡是很常見的支付方式，買衣服、買雜貨可以刷卡，有的地方甚至連付停車費、繳罰單都能刷卡呢！要表達刷卡或付現的方式，take 是個很好用的動詞，在這個語境中表示「接受」的意思。因此，「付現」就是 take cash。

• 關於「支付」，你還能這樣說：

Can I pay by credit card?

我可以刷卡嗎？

Can I have a receipt please?

可以給我收據嗎？

Do you have contactless?

你們有感應式支付嗎？

receipt 收據	contactless 感應式支付

7. What time are you open till?　你們營業到幾點？

> till 直到

台灣的生活相當便利，大部分的店家都很遲才關門，但許多國外的店家常常過了晚飯時間就歇業了，或逢假日公休。因此，我們最好跟店家確認清楚營業時間，才不會白跑一趟喔！本句中的 open 是作為形容詞，表示「開業的」。

- 關於「詢問營業時間」，你還能這樣說：

What time do you close today?
你們今天幾點關店？

What are your opening hours?
請問你們的營業時間是……？

Are you open on the weekends?
你們週末營業嗎？

opening hours 營業時間

8. What do you think of the jeans? 你覺得這條牛仔褲如何？

think of 想到／jeans 牛仔褲

跟三五好友逛街時常常需要身旁的「軍師」來幫忙出謀策劃，幫自己的品味把把關，以免買到雷人的商品。其中，最常用到的句子就是 What do you think of...？但小心不要講成 How do you think of...？了喔！這是錯誤的用法。

- 關於「詢問他人意見」，你還能這樣說：

Can you give me any suggestions?
你可以給我一點建議嗎？

Which one suits me better?
哪一個更適合我？

Which one do you prefer?
你更喜歡哪一個？

suggestion 建議	suit 適合	prefer 更喜歡

9. It's a bargain. 真划算。

bargain 便宜的價格

中文講的「殺價」，英文可不是 killing the price 喔！而是用 bargain 這個字。bargain 作為名詞時，原指「便宜貨」，也能引伸為「划算的價格」的意思。下次當你買到物美價廉的東西時，發自內心的來一句：It's a bargain. 吧！

- 關於「划算」，你還能這樣說：

It's a steal.
真划算。

That's a good buy.
真划算。

That cost next to nothing.
那簡直不用錢。

steal 贓物（以低價買到的東西）	next to 接近

10. That's highway robbery. 那簡直是搶劫！

highway 高速公路／**robbery** 搶劫

買東西時難免遇到不肖賣家漫天開價，有時候開得價格簡直不合理到極點，有時候消費者沒有貨比三家還真的容易吃悶虧。這種情形就像是「在高速公路上的攔車搶劫」一樣，光天化日，明目張膽地搶劫。如果有朋友跟你抱怨東西買貴了，你就可以回：That's highway robbery!

- 關於「太貴了」，你還能這樣說：

That's a rip-off.
太坑了。

That's a bit steep.
那真有點貴。

I paid through the nose to dine in that fancy restaurant.
在那間高級餐廳吃飯花了我好多錢。

rip-off 剝削	**steep** 昂貴的	**pay through one's nose** 花很多錢
dine 用餐	**fancy** 高檔的	

 與購物有關的慣用語：

1. off the market 不是單身狀態

哈哈：You should stop chasing after Craig. He's off the market.
妳別再追求 Craig 了。他已經死會了。

Lyla：No! I just can't let go.
不！我放不下他！

2. shopping therapy 購物治療法

哈哈：Oh my goodness! Why did you buy so many things?
天啊！妳怎麼買這麼多東西？

Lyla：I was upset, so I needed some shopping therapy.
我心情不好，需要來點購物治療。

3. cost a fortune 非常貴

哈哈：How much does your new sofa cost?
妳的新沙發多少錢？

Lyla：Well. It cost a fortune, but it's totally worth it.
嗯，超貴的！但完全值得！

4. shop till you drop　買到升天

哈哈：I'm so excited about the trip to London.

　　　要去倫敦我超興奮的！

Lyla：Yeah! You will shop till you drop. So sleep tight tonight.

　　　嗯哼！你會買到升天的！所以今晚好好睡吧！

5. window shopping　櫥窗購物（只看不買的購物行程）

哈哈：Wanna go shopping later?

　　　今天想去買東西嗎？

Lyla：Well, I can only go window shopping. I haven't got paid.

　　　我只能櫥窗購物欸！我還沒發薪水。

第4章 哈啦剪髮

角色：哈哈（來自台灣）、Lyla（來自美國）

在國外剪頭髮一直是件困擾人的事,除了東、西方人髮質、造型方式相差甚遠外,如何用英文溝通自己的需求才是更大的問題。尤其當自己對髮型的要求比較高時,在很多技術細節的語言傳達上又大大增加了難度。今天我們就來學學非常實用的剪髮英文會話,往後出國也可以大膽走進理髮店囉!

1. Can you fit me in for a haircut at 3 p.m. tomorrow?

你可以幫我預約明天下午三點的剪髮嗎?

> fit sb. in 為某人安排預約／ haircut 剪髮

「預約」除了 make a reservation 之外,還可以說:book 和 fit me in for...。其中,fit in 的意思就是「安插進去……」。如果是和某位設計師約時間,我們則可以用 make an appointment with「與……預約」。若你是第一次上這間理髮店,想詢問價錢,你可以問:How much do you charge for a...?「請問你們……多少錢?」

- 關於「預約理髮」,你還能這樣說:

  Hi. I'd like to book a wash and cut.
  你好,我想預約洗加剪。

  Good morning. Can I make an appointment with Freddy for a perm tomorrow?
  早安,我想預約明天找 Freddy 做燙髮。

  Would Andy be available tomorrow afternoon?
  Andy 老師明天下午有空嗎?

book 預約	wash 洗髮	cut 剪髮
appointment 預約	perm 燙髮	available 有空的

2. I'd like a wash and cut.　我要洗加剪。

> wash　洗髮／ cut　剪髮

走進理髮店時，我們首先需要回答幾個常見的問題：What can I do for you today?「今天需要什麼服務？」、Do you have a reservation?「您有預約嗎？」、Do you have your own stylist?「您有指定設計師嗎？」、Would you like some tea or coffee?「您要來點茶或咖啡嗎？」

- 關於「進理髮廳」，你還能這樣說：

  I have an appointment with George.
  我約了 George 老師。

  No. It's my first time here. Can you recommend one for me?
  沒有，我第一次來，你可以幫我推薦一下嗎？

  Yes, coffee, please. Thank you very much.
  咖啡好了，謝謝！

appointment　預約	recommend　推薦

3. I don't mind waiting a little bit.　我等一下沒關係。

> mind　介意

有時候，即使事前預約了，也會因為設計師太忙或各種原因需要在現場等待。這時候，接待人員可能會說：We'll be with you in a minute.「我們等一下就來。」或先讓設計師助理帶你去洗頭髮。這時候，我們就可以用上以下相關的對話。

- 關於「剪髮準備」，你還能這樣說：

  Excuse me. How much longer do I have to wait?
  不好意思，請問我還需要等多久？

  The water is too hot.
  水太熱了。

You can rub harder.

你可以按大力一點。

---

rub 按摩

---

4. I just want a trim all over. 我想要全部稍微修剪一下就好。

> **trim** 修剪／ **all over** 全部

設計師就位時，通常會說：How would you like your hair cut? 或 What would you like to have done today?「今天想要做什麼造型？」如果要「些微修剪」我們可以用 trim 這個字。另外，trim off the top ／ the sides ／ the back ／ the bangs 意思便是「修剪頭頂／兩側／後面／瀏海」。如果想剪短一點，我們可以說：I want it shorter this time. 或 I'd like it shorter this time.「我這次想剪短一點。」這個句型：I want it V-pp. 或 I'd like it V-pp. 可以套用所有的造型動詞，非常好用喔！

[註]：其他造型的英文：thin 打薄／ layer 剪層次／ color 染色／ bleach 漂白／ dye 染色／ highlight 挑染／ perm 燙／ curl 捲／ straighten 拉直／ shave 剃光

- 關於「溝通需求（一）」，你還能這樣說：

I want something like this in the picture.
我想要剪成照片裡的這樣。

I'd like to keep the length.
我想要保持長度。

I want a more energetic look this time.
我這次想要剪得比較有精神一點。

---

length 長度　　　**energetic** 有精神的

---

5. I'm thinking of getting a perm. Can you give me some suggestions?　我在想要不要燙髮，你可以給我一點建議嗎？

> perm　燙髮／ suggestion　建議

如果自己對造型比較沒概念或拿不定主意時，可以諮詢一下設計師，讓他們推薦適合你的造型。我們可以問：Can you recommend a hairstyle for me? 你可以推薦一下適合我的髮型嗎？如果自己在考慮燙髮，但仍需要一點建議，我們可以問：I'm thinking of getting a perm. Can you give me some suggestions?「我在考慮要不要燙髮，你可以給我一點建議嗎？」其中，I'm thinking of... 便是「我在考慮……。」最後，如果我們對設計師的建議很滿意，想嘗試看看時，我們可以說：Sounds good. I'll go for that. 或 Let's do it!「聽起來不錯！那就這樣剪吧！」

• 關於「溝通需求（二）」，你還能這樣說：

Can you give my hair more body?
你可以把我的頭髮弄蓬一點嗎？

Would you suggest straightening it on top?
你會建議把上面拉直嗎？

I'd like to get my hair dyed. What color would you suggest?
我想要染髮，你有推薦什麼顏色嗎？

body　體積	suggest　建議	straighten　拉直
inch　英吋		

6. I want my fringe just above my eyebrows.
我想要瀏海剪到眉毛上面一點。

> fringe　瀏海／ above　在……上面／ eyebrows　眉毛

接著，我們來學關於更細節的造型需求。如果想要頭髮剪到某個指定的長度，我們可以說：I want it just above my...「我想要剪到……以上的地方。」如果想要表達「剪掉多少長度」，最簡單的就是用比的，先比出一個長度，然後說：I'd like this taken off.「我想要剪掉這麼多。」關於染髮，如果想「染淺一點」，可

以説：I want it lighter.，「染深一點」，則是 I want it darker.。最後，關於髮線的分法，「中分」是 center part，「旁分」是 side part。

- 關於「溝通需求（三）」，你還能這樣説：

I want it to stand out.
我想要顏色明顯一點。

I'd like an inch taken off on the sides.
我想要兩邊都剪掉一吋。

I'd like to get a side part.
我想要旁分。

stand out 明顯	inch 英吋	sides 側邊
side part 旁分		

7. I think bangs are really difficult to maintain.
我覺得瀏海好難整理。

> bangs 瀏海／maintain 維持

通常剪頭髮時，設計師會跟你天南地北的瞎聊，聊工作、聊興趣、聊時事……，如果真的不知道要聊什麼，既然你都在理髮店了，那就聊聊頭髮吧！

- 關於「頭髮的大小事」，你還能這樣説：

I've never got highlights before.
我從來沒有挑染過。

My hair grows super fast.
我的頭髮長超快的。

The last time I got my hair cut was probably five months ago.
我上次剪頭髮大概是五個月前。

highlights 挑染	probably 可能

8. I think I look so weird with tight curls.　我覺得我燙小卷好奇怪。

> weird 奇怪的／tight curls 小卷

關於髮型，我們必須學一個常用的動詞 wear。wear 的原意是「穿戴」，但也可以用在髮型上。比如：wear a pony tail「綁馬尾」、wear an afro「燙黑人爆炸頭」等。另外，我們也需要學一個介系詞 with。with 也有「穿戴」的意思，比如：You will look good with waves.「你燙大波浪會很好看。」

- 關於「各種髮型」，你還能這樣說：

  I don't have a good head shape to go bald.
  我的頭型不好看，不能理光頭。

  I always wear my hair in braids.
  我一直都綁辮子。

  I'd like an updo.
  我想要整頭盤上去。

head shape　頭型	bald　光頭	braid　辮子
updo　頭髮上盤		

9. My hair gets tangled a lot.　我的頭髮常常打結。

> tangled 打結的

理髮店常會跟某特定品牌的洗髮、保養產品合作，並幫他們推銷，我們當然可以說 Thanks. I'll think about that.「謝謝，我會考慮一下。」但如果自己的頭髮真的需要特殊的護理時，不妨考慮諮詢一下專業理髮師的意見喔！

- 關於「頭髮的問題」，你還能這樣說：

  My hair is very frizzy. How can I get it fixed?
  我的頭髮很毛躁，請問要怎麼解決呢？

  How do I get rid of my split ends?
  我怎麼解決我髮尾分岔的問題呢？

What kind of shampoo would you recommend for oily hair?

針對油性髮質你推薦哪一種洗髮乳？

frizzy 毛躁的	fix 修理	get rid of 去除
split ends 髮尾分岔	shampoo 洗髮乳	oily 油膩的

10. It looks perfect. Thank you so much. 太完美了，謝謝你！

> perfect 完美的

剪完頭髮後，設計師會問：Do you want to use a mirror?「你要用鏡子看一下嗎？」如果看完之後非常滿意，我們可以說：It looks perfect／wonderful／fantastic.「非常好。」有些地方有給設計師小費的習慣，記得入境隨俗一下喔！

• 關於「剪髮完畢」，你還能這樣說：

This is exactly what I wanted.
這完全就是我想要的。

It's all right.
很好！

I guess it will take time for me to get used to it.
我可能要過陣子才能習慣它吧！

exactly 正是	get used to 習慣

• 跟剪髮有關的慣用語

1. split hairs 鑽牛角尖

哈哈：I'm still deciding if I should cut my bangs.
我還在糾結要不要剪瀏海。

Lyla：To me, it doesn't matter. Don't you think you're splitting hairs?
對我來說沒差，你不覺得你在鑽牛角尖嗎？

2. **get into one's hair**　惹毛某人

哈哈：You know...it's really hard to decide. Do you think I should cut it?

真的好難抉擇喔！妳覺得到底要不要剪啊？

Lyla：You're getting into my hair. Cut it!

你惹毛我了！剪吧！

3. **get out of one's hair**　遠離某人

哈哈：I messed up with my bangs. I shouldn't have cut it myself.

我的瀏海剪壞了，我真不應該自己剪的。

Lyla：Get out of my hair. You don't look any different with or without your bangs.

走開啦！你有沒有瀏海看起來都一樣。

4. **let your hair down**　放開來玩

哈哈：Mid-term's finally over! Let's let your hair down and unwire yourself.

期中考終於結束了，讓我們一起放飛玩耍吧！

Lyla：I have another mid-term coming up next week.

我下週還有一個期中考。

5. **win by a hair**　以些微差距險勝

哈哈：Let's get the game started! I am gonna crush you big time.

開始比賽吧！我會擊垮妳的！

Lyla：Cut the crap! You only won by a hair last time.

少來了！你上次只贏我一點點而已。

第 5 章 哈啦看病

角色：哈哈（來自台灣）、Lyla（來自美國）

很多人在國外很怕去看醫生，一來是因為國外的醫療費用高昂、醫病文化不同，二來是無法用英文準確地說明自己的症狀和感受。其實，看病時只需要將自己的症狀概要、細節、出現的部位、時間和頻率簡單扼要地說明清楚，傳達給醫護人員就行了，並不需要很深奧的醫學詞彙。看病前最好先梳理一下思路，或把該跟醫生說的點寫下來，才不會到看診時因為太緊張漏講了某個點，讓醫生誤判了那就麻煩大囉！

1. You don't look well. I think you should go and see a doctor.

你看起來不太舒服，我覺得你要去看個醫生。

> well 健康的／ see a doctor 看醫生

身邊的人看起來不對勁時，我們可以說：You don't look well.「你看起來不太舒服。」well 在本句中是當形容詞，意思是「健康的」，跟 You did well. 的 well 作為副詞不一樣。而建議別人去就醫，我們可以說：I think you should go and see a doctor.「我覺得你要去看個醫生。」其中的 go and see 結構是英語口語中很常見的用法，意思和 go to see 沒什麼區別，比如：I'm gonna go and check if they have any problems.「我要去看一下他們有沒有問題。」

• 關於「需要就醫」，你還能這樣說：

I've been fighting a cold for three days. I want to see a doctor.
我已經感冒三天了，我想要去看醫生。

I need to go to the doctor and get my shoulder looked at.
我需要去看醫生檢查一下我的肩膀。

My leg hurts. I will go get it checked out at a hospital.
我的腿好痛，我要去醫院檢查一下。

hurt 痛	check up 檢查

2. Good morning. I'd like to make an appointment to see Dr. Johnson, please. 早安，我想預約和 Johnson 醫生看診。

appointment 預約

國外很少有醫院或診所接受 walk-in「沒有預約」，因此，看病或健診前一定得預約。「和……醫生預約看診」我們可以說：make an appointment with Dr. ... 此時，護士或助理可能會問你：Have you been in to see Dr. …before?「您之前有來看診過嗎？」、May I have your name, please?「請問您的大名是？」、What seems to be the problem?「什麼地方不舒服？」等。關於安排掛號，還可能會說到：There's a slot available at six in the evening.「晚上六點有一個時段可以。」、We have a four o'clock opening today.「我們今天四點有一個時段可以。」、I can fit you in tomorrow morning.「我幫您掛明天早上的號。」

• 關於「預約看診」，你還能這樣說：

I'm afraid I won't be able to make that appointment. I get off work at six.
那個時間我可能沒辦法，我六點下班。

I prefer to take today's appointment.
我比較想掛號今天的門診。

Do you take appointments after 6 pm?
你們六點之後可以預約嗎？

make 趕到	get off work 下班	prefer 更喜歡

3. I'm here to see Dr. Johnson. 我跟 Johnson 醫生預約了看診。

see 看診

到達醫院或診所時，通常需要跟櫃檯人員表明來訪目的，並詢問病房或診間在哪。如果是自己看病，我們可以說：I'm here to see Dr. ...，如果是去探病，我們可以說：I'm here to visit...。至於醫院的「部門」則是：ward 或 department。如果是大醫院，還會有分 wing「側廳」，比如：east wing「東側」或 west wing

「西側」。其他常見的部門還有：A & E (Accident and Emergency)「急診室」、ICU (Intensive Care Unit)「加護病房」、laboratory「檢驗室」、X-ray room「X光室」、delivery room「產房」、outpatient clinic「門診部」、inpatient ward「住院部」、pharmacy「藥局」。

> [註]：其他醫院部門的英文：ENT department 耳鼻喉科／ dentistry department 牙科／ dermatology department 皮膚科／ family medicine department 家庭醫學科／ obstetrics and gynaecology department 婦產科／ neurology department 神經內科／ ophthalmology department 眼科／ pediatric department 小兒科／ oncology department 腫瘤科／ urology department 泌尿科

• 關於「到達醫院」，你還能這樣說：

Hi. I have an appointment with Dr. Seaberg.
你好，我跟 Seaberg 醫生約了看診。

I'm here to visit my sister.
我來探望我妹妹的。

Excuse me. Where's the children's ward?
請問兒童病房在哪裡？

visit 探望	ward 病房

4. I have a terrible ache in my lower back.　我的下背好痛。

ache 痛／ lower 下部的

進入診間後，當醫生問你：What brings you here today?「今天怎麼了？」時，先用一句話大略地描述你的症狀，如：I have a stomach problem.「我肚子不舒服。」或 I have a terrible ache in my...「我的⋯⋯很痛。」讓醫生有一個大致的方向。

• 關於「報告症狀」，你還能這樣說：

I feel a bit nauseous.
我感覺有點噁心。

I'm having trouble breathing.
我呼吸困難。

My chest feels tight.
我胸悶。

nauseous 噁心的	breathe 呼吸	chest 胸
tight 緊的		

5. I've been experiencing throbbing pain on the back of my shoulders. 我的肩膀後面最近會一陣一陣地痛。

experience 經歷／ throbbing 顫動的／ pain 疼痛／ shoulder 肩膀

報告完大致問題後，再根據自身的實際情形描述症狀發生的位置、時間、頻率及狀況等細節，盡可能誠實、明確地描述，或搭配動作、手指部位等，讓醫生有足夠的資訊來進行診斷。如：The back of my shoulders has throbbing pain. 「我的肩膀後面會一陣陣地痛。」其中，描述疼痛有幾種説法：dull pain「鈍痛」、sharp pain「刺痛」、piercing pain「刺痛」、intense pain「劇痛」。

[註]：其他常見症狀的英文：fever 發燒／ cough 咳嗽／ productive cough 咳嗽有痰／ dry cough 乾咳／ runny nose 流鼻水／ stuffy nose 鼻塞／ sore throat 喉嚨痛／ itchy throat 喉嚨癢／ sneezing 打噴嚏／ headache 頭痛／ stomachache 肚痛／ nausea 噁心／ vomiting 嘔吐／ diarrhea 腹瀉／ tightness 緊／ weakness 虛弱無力／ fatigue 疲勞／ dizziness 暈眩／ lightheadedness 頭昏眼花／ shortness of breath 呼吸困難

• 關於「描述症狀（一）」，你還能這樣説：

I get a bad headache in the morning, especially on cold days, and it usually lasts for a while.
我早上都會頭痛，尤其是天氣冷的時候，而且通常會持續一陣子。

My temperature spiked up to 38 degrees last night.
我的體溫昨天晚上飆到三十八度。

It comes and goes.
它時好時壞的。

especially 尤其	temperature 體溫	spike 飆升
degree 度	come and go 來來去去	

6. I started to have this sore throat two days ago and it got worse this morning. 我喉嚨兩天前開始痛的，到今天早上更嚴重了。

sore throat 喉嚨痛／worse 更糟的

除了症狀發生的部位、時間，症狀的變化情形也很關鍵，特別是複診時，醫生需要追蹤病症的發展，此時，精準的傳達能力就尤為重要了。關於「變好」、「變糟」，我們可以說：get better、get worse。而症狀「消失」、「復發」則可以簡單用 go away、come back again 來表示。

• 關於「描述症狀（二）」，你還能這樣說：

I feel better when I take some aspirin, but it comes back again after a few hours.
我吃阿斯匹靈之後會感覺好一點，但幾個小時之後又會復發。

It's been easing up a little. Looks like the medication is working.
最近好多了，看來藥物有起作用。

My neck feels fine unless I turn my head quickly and I will feel a sharp pain.
我的脖子只有在我很快地轉頭的時候會感覺到一陣刺痛。

aspirin 阿斯匹靈	ease up 減緩	medication 藥物
work 起作用	unless 除非	sharp 尖銳的

7. What is it that's causing my symptoms?
請問我的症狀是什麼造成的？

cause 造成／symptom 症狀

除了要會報告病症狀況，詢問的技巧也不能不學。包含：病症起因、手術細節及其他注意事項等。詢問病症起因，我們可以用以下的句型：

What is it that's causing my...?「請問我的…是什麼造成的？」做手術前，怕痛的人可能會問：「手術會痛嗎？」這句的英文是：Is it gonna hurt? 而當醫生說到手術無大礙時，經常我們會說：That's a relief!「真是鬆了一口氣！」

- 關於「諮詢醫師」，你還能這樣說：

Is there anything I should avoid doing during the treatment?
治療期間我需要避免什麼嗎？

What side effects should I watch for with the surgery?
做這個手術會有什麼副作用？

Is there anything else that I need to take care of?
我還需要注意什麼嗎？

avoid 避免	treatment 治療	side effect 副作用
watch for 注意	surgery 手術	

8. I was under general anesthesia, so I was completely unconscious. 我做了全身麻醉，所以我完全沒有意識。

general anesthesia 全身麻醉／ completely 完全地／ unconscious 無意識的

治療結束後，我們常常會和親朋好友描述治療過程，包含麻醉、縫針、吊點滴及各種儀器等。其中，「麻醉」的名詞為 anesthesia，動詞為 anesthesize，「全身麻醉」為 general anesthesia，「局部麻醉」為 partial anesthesia。與 anesthesia 搭配的介系詞為 under。而「裝上某某儀器」，英文是用介系詞 on 來表示，比如：on a drip「吊點滴」、on a ventilator「戴氧氣罩」等。

- 關於「描述治療過程」，你還能這樣說：

I had seven stitches on my underarm.
我腋下縫了七針。

I was on a drip at the hospital for three days.
我去醫院吊點滴吊了三天。

I was put on a ventilator and I was hooked up to every machine and I was like what's going on!?

我被戴上氧氣罩，身體被接上各種機器，我當時想：到底怎麼了！？

stitch 縫針	underarm 腋下	on a drip 吊點滴
ventilator 氧氣罩	hook up 連接上	

9. Do I need to be admitted?　我需要住院嗎？

admit 使住院

admit 和 hospitalize 都是「使住院」的意思，因此，be admitted to the hospital 和 be hospitalized 都可以表示「住院」。或者我們可以用更簡單明瞭的說法，如：I'll have to spend the night in the hospital.「我今天晚上要住院。」或 They said I'll need overnight observation in the hospital.「他們說我今天必須住院觀察。」

• 關於「住院」，你還能這樣說：

How long will I be in the hospital?
我需要住院多久？

I'm feeling a lot better. I should be getting out soon.
我好多了，應該快出院了。

Hopefully I'll be discharged soon.
希望我可以早點出院。

hopefully 希望	discharge 使出院

10. I'm not feeling well today and need to take a day off to recover. I'll be back in tomorrow. Thank you for your understanding.　我今天不舒服，需要請假休息一天。我明天就可以進公司了。謝謝您的理解。

well 健康的／ take a day off 請一天假／ recover 恢復／ understanding 理解

最後，我們來學學如何請病假。請病假的關鍵：明確表達原因、語氣委婉而堅定、態度有禮。另外，別忘了也表達一下自己的敬業態度，讓主管覺得：即使臥病在床也心繫工作，這樣的病假肯定可以請得更順利喔！

- 關於「請病假」，你還能這樣說：

I woke up this morning feeling pretty ill and I think it' best for me to take the day off and rest up.
我今天早上醒來感覺很不舒服，我覺得我最好請個假休息一下。

I'm sorry for any inconvenience, but my daughter fell ill this morning and has been running a temperature and I need to take her to the doctor, so I may have to use a sick day.
不好意思造成任何不便，我女兒今天早上生病了，現在一直在發燒，我得帶她去看醫生，所以我可能需要請個假。

I think I've come down with the flu, so I'll be staying home from work today. I'll try to be on Line as much as I can.
我覺得我可能得流感了，所以今天會請假待在家，但我會盡量在 Line 上待命。

ill 生病的	rest 休息	inconvenience 不便
fall ill 生病	run a temperature 發燒	sick day 病假
come down with 患有……		

 跟看病有關的慣用語

1. under the weather 生病

哈哈：What's wrong with you? You look as pale as a ghost.
妳怎麼了？臉色好蒼白？

Lyla：I'm under the weather. I may need to call in sick today.
我不舒服，今天可能要請假一下。

2. be sick as a dog　病懨懨

哈哈：I haven't seen you for the past two days. What happened to you?

我這兩天都沒有看到妳，怎麼了啊？

Lyla：You didn't know that? I was sick as a dog. I almost puked my guts out yesterday.

你不知道嗎？我病得超嚴重的，我昨天差點把腸胃都吐出來了。

3. not quite oneself　不在狀態

哈哈：Oh…what's wrong with me? I'm not quite myself today. I may be sick.

喔……我怎麼了？我今天不在狀態，可能生病了。

Lyla：Yes. You always are.

嗯……你一直都有病。

4. go under the knife　動手術

哈哈：So what did the doctor say?

所以醫生怎麼說？

Lyla：Get it removed. I'll have to go under the knife.

把它拿掉。我必須動手術了。

5. alive and kicking　生龍活虎

哈哈：How are you doing? Feeling better?

妳還好嗎？好點了沒？

Lyla：Yeah…alive and kicking again! I'll be back in tomorrow.

嗯嗯……我又滿血復活了，明天就能回去上班了。

第6章 哈啦美食

角色：哈哈（來自台灣）、Lyla（來自美國）

台灣的夜市小吃名聞遐邇，但有些真的會讓歐美遊客望之卻步，像是：臭豆腐、滷雞爪、豬血糕、棺材板，一個個彷彿來自地獄的食物，光是聽名字就讓人嚇破膽。這時，如果英語又不夠好，無法忠實地描述這些小吃的美味，那可真的會讓外國友人把台灣小吃列入黑名單呢！以下哈啦美食十金句，讓你能夠暢聊美食不 NG。

1. It looks very delicate.　看起來好精緻。

> delicate　精緻的

色、香、味，色字總是擺第一位！不管是網紅餐廳的精緻甜品，還是夜市小吃的粗礪美食，光是外觀就讓人食指大動，垂涎三尺。尤其現在人手一支高像素拍照手機，「手機先開動」儼然已成為一種神聖的餐前儀式。而當我們在跟國外友人討論美食的顏值時，最簡單、最常用的句子便是：It looks...。

• 關於「描述食物外觀」，你還能這樣說：

It looks so rich!
看起來好飽滿！

Amazing plating!
擺盤好讚！

It doesn't look appealing, but it tastes pretty good.
它看起來不怎麼吸引人，但嚐起來挺好的。

rich　飽實的	plating　擺盤	appealing　吸引人的

2. It smells so good.　好香啊！

> smell　聞起來

美食當前，最能催人食慾的莫過於撲鼻而來的香氣了。找不到合適的「香」的英文單字嗎？你可能學過 fragrant、aromatic⋯ 但其實，最簡單的說法就是 It smells good.。

- 關於「描述食物氣味」，你還能這樣說：

It smells like mustard.
這聞起來像芥末。

What is that pungent smell?
那是什麼刺鼻的氣味啊？

It smells interesting.
這氣味好微妙。

| mustard 芥末 | pungent 刺鼻的 | interesting 微妙的 |

3. It is crispy on the outside, fluffy on the inside.　它外酥內軟。

crispy 酥脆的／ outside 外層／ fluffy 鬆軟的／ inside 內層

大口咬下美食，總要説説口感如何，給觀眾一個交代吧！想要説得生動又有層次，不妨試試這句：It's...on the outside, ...on the inside. 而我們一般最常説的外酥內軟，酥脆我們可以説：crispy、crunchy、crusty，軟嫩我們則可以説：fluffy、soft、puffy。

- 關於「口感」，你還能這樣說：

The bread has a chewy texture.
這個麵包口感很 Q 彈。

The filling is very thick and creamy.
這內餡非常濃厚。

This really melts in the mouth.
入口即化。

| chewy 有嚼勁的 | texture 質地 | filling 內餡 |
| thick 厚實 | creamy 奶狀的 | melt 融化 |

4. The soup is just too bland. 這湯味道太淡了。

bland 口味淡的

美食味道千百種，身為饕客的我們為了忠實呈現食物的味道，當然不能只會簡單的 sweet、salty、sour 和 spicy 啦！這幾句學起來，不怕描述美味時詞窮了！

• 關於「描述食物味道」，你還能這樣說：

The coffee is full-flavored.
這咖啡味道很濃郁。

It's so well-seasoned.
這個調味調得真好。

The chicken wings are hot and spicy.
這些雞翅很辣。

[註]：hot 是指辣椒產生的辣味，而 spicy 則是指其他辛香料的味道。

full-flavored 味道濃郁的	well-seasoned 調味調得好的	chicken wing 雞翅
spicy 香辣的		

5. It's very delicious. 非常好吃！

delicious 美味的

形容食物好吃的說法很多種，除了 It's delicious. 之外，還可以說 It's really good. ／ It's great. ／ It's yummy. ／ It's very tasty. 等。更文雅的說法還有：It's palatable. ／ It's delectable.

• 關於「美味的說法」，你還能這樣說：

I love how flavorful the paella is.
這海鮮燉飯真好吃。

They make such mouth-watering cakes.
他們的蛋糕超好吃。

I can't get enough of their spaghetti.
我永遠吃不膩他們的義大利麵。

flavorful 美味的	paella 海鮮燉飯	mouth-watering 令人流口水的
can't have enough of 吃不膩	spaghetti 義大利麵	

6. It's not my cup of tea.　它不是我的菜。

not one's cup of tea　不是某人所喜愛的

有些地方特色美食不是人人都能接受的，當朋友熱情介紹的美食我們不太鍾意時，我們可以委婉地說：I think it is very interesting, but it's just not my cup of tea.

• 關於「吐槽食物」，你還能這樣說：

I'm not a big fan of seafood.
我不太吃海鮮。

It's revolting. Just to look at it.
看著就覺得好噁心啊！

The bacon is overcooked.
這培根烤過頭了。

be a big fan of 很喜歡……	revolting 令人作嘔的	overcooked 烹煮過頭了的

7. What is this made of?　這是什麼做的？

> be made of　由……製成

吃到新奇的美食，總會好奇它們是由什麼做成的。這時候我們就可以問：What is this made of? 但有時候，好吃就好，至於是什麼做的，不要問，嘿嘿！

- 關於「詢問食物由什麼製成的」，你還能這樣說：

Is this beef?

這是牛肉嗎？

What is that crunchy thing in the middle?

中間脆脆的東西是什麼？

Looking at the color, I'll bet it has turmeric in it.

看它的顏色，我賭裡面一定有加薑黃。

crunchy 脆的	turmeric 薑黃

8. It is deep-fried.　這是油炸的。

> deep-fried　油炸的

聊到食物的烹調方式時，通常我們會用動詞的過去分詞作為形容詞來表達。
deep-fried 的中文意思是「油炸的」，而一般我們為求方便會縮略成 fried，然而，
fried 狹義上是表示「煎」、「炒」，與 deep-fried 的區別就是 deep-fried 放的
油比較多。

[註]：其他十種烹製方式：stir-fried 炒的／ pan-fried 煎的／ steamed 蒸的／ baked
烘焙的／ roasted 烤的／ grilled 烤的（放烤架上）／ stewed 燉的／ simmered
煨的／ braised 魯的／ marinated 醃的。

- 關於「食物的烹製方式」，你還能這樣說：

I would like my steak medium-well.

我的牛排想要七分熟。

[註]：其他牛排熟度：raw 生的／ medium-rare 三分熟／ medium 五分熟／ well-done
全熟

I like how the fried rice is cooked so evenly.
我喜歡這炒飯粒粒分明。

The fish fillet is slightly undercooked.
這個魚排有點生。

steak 牛排	medium-well 七分熟	fried rice 炒飯
evenly 平均的	fillet 肉片	slightly 稍微地
undercooked 未煮熟的		

9. The chicken really goes well with the potatoes.
這雞肉真的跟馬鈴薯好搭！

> go well with 與……很配

吃到絕配的美食組合真的會給人上天堂的感覺呢！這時不來句道地的英文句子表揚一下怎麼行呢！這裡介紹一句很好用的 go well with，不管是美食、穿搭或其他事物的搭配都能用上這句喔！

• 關於「食物的搭配」，你還能這樣說：

Bacon and eggs are a perfect match.
培根和雞蛋真是絕配！

Burgers and fries are the best food duo ever.
漢堡和薯條是史上最搭的食物了。

Pizza and pineapples simply don't go together.
披薩和鳳梨簡直太不搭了。

bacon 培根	match 搭配	fries 薯條
duo 一對	go together 搭配得好	

10. This is no doubt the best sushi I've ever had.

這是我吃過最好吃的壽司了。

> no doubt 無疑／ sushi 壽司

有人說過，當你不知道要聊什麼的時候，就聊聊吃的吧！關於吃的經驗相信許多人都能滔滔不絕、如數家珍。在大家最愛的「吃」的話題上，我們當然不能因為破破的英文阻斷了話題的開展。因此，不管是破冰話題，還是初嚐美食後的真情流露，你都需要幾句道地的英文句子來 carry 你。其中，the best...I've ever had 是最常見的句型之一了，用來描述各種經驗都很合適喔！

• 關於「吃的經驗」，你還能這樣說：

I've never eaten anything like this before.
我從來沒有吃過這種東西。

I've always loved Chinese food.
我一直都很喜歡中國菜。

I'm a huge fan of seafood.
我超愛吃海鮮。

huge 巨大的	seafood 海鮮

 跟吃有關的慣用語

1. eat like a horse　食慾很好

Lyla：Look at you. You're eating like a horse.
　　　看看你，食慾這麼好！

哈哈：I haven't eaten for two days.
　　　我兩天沒吃飯了。

2. **one's cup of tea**　是……喜歡、擅長的人事物

哈哈：How did your lesson go?
　　　妳的課上得怎麼樣啊？

Lyla：It was a mess. Teaching isn't really my cup of tea.
　　　一團糟。我真的不擅長教書。

3. **make a pig of oneself**　吃得太多

哈哈：I made a pig of myself at dinner.
　　　我今天晚餐吃太多了。

Lyla：I thought you always are a pig.
　　　你不是一直都是隻豬嗎？

4. **chew the fat**　閒聊

哈哈：What were you and your mother talking about?
　　　妳那時候在跟妳媽說什麼啊？

Lyla：Nothing. We were just chewing the fat.
　　　沒什麼，我們只是在閒聊。

5. **have one's cake and eat it**　魚與熊掌兼得

哈哈：I can't stand her nagging, but feel lonely when she's not here.
　　　我受不了她的喋喋不休，但她不在這裡時我又覺得很寂寞。

Lyla：Well, you can't have your cake and eat it.
　　　魚與熊掌不可兼得啊！

第 7 章 哈啦外食

角色：哈哈（來自台灣）、Lyla（來自美國）

不管是出國旅行還是帶外國友人來台灣玩，上餐廳吃飯絕對是必備的行程。這時便是考驗我們英語交際能力的大好時機，從詢問、推薦餐廳，到訂位、點餐、結帳，每個環節都極其考驗我們的英語水平。此時，練就一口流利的英語，不僅能在點餐時讓友人刮目相看，也能避免因為語言不通而點錯餐的尷尬場面喔！

1. Can you recommend a restaurant around here?
你可以推薦一下附近的餐廳嗎？

recommend 推薦／ restaurant 餐廳

想找網紅餐廳卻懶得做攻略嗎？不妨試試廣大朋友圈的 word of mouth「口耳相傳」，直接問問家人、朋友或同事們，有時候往往更能找到真正五星好評的餐館喔！

• 關於「推薦餐廳」，你還能這樣說：

What is the best restaurant to dine in Taichung?
台中最棒的餐廳是哪間？

What are the must-eat restaurants in Seattle?
西雅圖必吃的餐廳有哪些？

You have to go to Super Duper. It has the best burgers in town.
你一定要去 Super Duper。那裡的漢堡是這裡最好吃的！

dine 用餐	must-eat 一定要吃的

2. I'd like to reserve a table for two for tonight at 5 pm.

我想預定今晚五點兩個人的位子。

> reserve 預訂

訂位通常是跟餐廳服務生打交道的第一關，並且通常是透過電話交談的，因此，能清楚地表達關鍵資訊，包含時間、人數及特別需求是很重要的。訂位英語的句式其實頗為固定，建議可以先把一個句子背起來，等熟練了之後再用其他句子增添點變化。在這個句型中，a table for... 表示「……人的座位」，其後的 for... 表示「訂……時間的位子」。

・ 關於「訂位」，你還能這樣說：

I need to make a dinner reservation for four for tomorrow evening.
我要訂明天晚餐四個人的位子。

I'd like to place a reservation for this coming Friday at six.
我想訂這星期五六點的位子。

I'd like to confirm a lunch reservation for four on August 15 under the name of Mark.
我想確認一下用馬克這個名字訂的八月十五日的四個人的午餐位子。

make a reservation 訂位	place a reservation 訂位	coming 即將到來的
confirm 確認	under the name of 以……的名字	

3. Hello. We haven't booked a table. Do you have a table available for two? 你好，我們沒有訂位，請問你們有兩人桌位嗎？

> book 預訂／available 有空的

很多時候我們上餐廳用餐也是臨時起意，沒有事先訂位。這個時候如何禮貌地跟服務員交涉、詢問桌位就考驗到我們的語用技巧了。怕臨場交談時緊張怯場嗎？還是那個建議：整句背下來吧！這句當中的 a table available 意思是「空的桌位」，我們也可以說：Do you have a table free for two?

第7章 哈啦外食

066

• 關於「詢問桌位」，你還能這樣說：

Excuse me. Would you be able to seat us now?
不好意思，請問你們現在還有桌位嗎？

We didn't make a reservation. Could you fit us in? There are four of us.
我們沒有訂位，你可以幫我們安排桌位嗎？我們有四位。

Do you have anything available for four at this moment?
請問你們現在有四人的桌位嗎？

seat 使入座	fit in 將……安排進去

4. Could you bring us the drinks menu, please?
可以給我們飲料的菜單嗎？

drinks 飲料／ menu 菜單

一般就餐入座後，便是開始物色餐點、選餐的時間。這時候可能會需要跟服務員要菜單、和朋友討論要點什麼，或請服務員推薦特色菜等。其中，要菜單除了上述例句之外，我們也可以這樣說：Could we see the menu, please?

[註]：其他種類的菜單：starters 前菜／ soups 湯／ main courses 主菜／ desserts 甜點

• 關於「討論選餐」，你還能這樣說：

What would you like to order?
你想點什麼？

Could you give us a few more minutes please?
可以再給我們幾分鐘看一下嗎？

What do you recommend?
你有推薦什麼菜嗎？

order 點菜	recommend 推薦

5. Can I have a chicken burger with garlic fries, please?

我想點一個雞肉堡和蒜味薯條。

> garlic 蒜

討論完畢，正式點餐了！首先，我們當然需要學會怎麼讀想點的菜名囉！如果真的不會讀，那也只能用一指神功，指哪點哪了！不過，就算菜名不會讀，點餐的基本句式總要學幾句起來的！ Can I have..., please? 應該是最簡單、最直接的句式了。

- 關於「點餐」，你還能這樣說：

I'd like (to order) an original lobster roll, please.
我想來一份原味龍蝦卷。

I'll have the clam chowder.
我點一份蛤蠣巧達濃湯。

May I get a glass of lemonade, please?
我想點一杯檸檬汁。

| original 原味的 | lobster 龍蝦 | roll 卷餅 |
| clam 蛤蠣 | chowder 巧達濃湯 | lemonade 檸檬汁 |

6. I'd like my noodles to be less spicy. 我的麵不要那麼辣。

> less 更不…… ／ spicy 辣的

相信每個人在飲食上多多少少都有一些特殊習慣或喜好，在外食時需要特別和服務員提醒一下，免得菜裡放了自己吃不來或不喜歡吃的東西，壞了用餐的興致。這句 I'd like my...to be... 意思就是「我的餐點需要做……的調整」。比如：
I'd like my steak to be well-done. 意思是「我的牛排要全熟。」；We'd like our desserts before the meal.「我們的甜點想要在餐前上。」

- 關於「餐點客製化需求」，你還能這樣說：

Can I have an iced coffee with no ice?
我可以來一份冰咖啡去冰嗎？

Is this dish suitable for vegans?

這道菜適合純素食者嗎？

Does this contain cilantro / coriander?

這道菜裡面有放香菜嗎？

iced 冰的	suitable 適合的	vegan 純素者
contain 包含	cilantro 香菜	coriander 香菜

7. Excuse me, sir. I didn't order the shrimp cake.

先生不好意思，我沒有點蝦餅喔。

> shrimp 蝦

外出用餐時難免會遇到送錯餐、上菜慢、菜涼了等問題，這幾句英文教你如何有禮貌又有效率地提出你的問題。其中，關於最常見的「送錯餐」，我們還可以說：I'm sorry, but I ordered...「不好意思，我點的是……。」

• 關於「用餐時出現的問題」，你還能這樣說：

I'm sorry, but my order hasn't arrived yet.

不好意思，我的餐還沒上。

Can you heat this soup up a little bit for me, please?

可以幫我的湯加熱一下嗎？

Excuse me. My fork dropped. Can you give me another one?

不好意思，我的叉子掉到地上了。可以給我一支新的嗎？

order 點菜	heat up 加熱	drop 掉落

8. Can I have one more jug of orange juice, please?

可以再給我一壺柳橙汁嗎？

> jug 壺

吃到美食總想無限續盤、續杯嗎？來學學加點餐點的兩大句式，以「我」開頭的 Can I have...? 和以「您」開頭的 Could you bring…?

• 關於「加點餐點」，你還能這樣說：

Could you bring me another glass of iced tea, please?
可以再給我一杯冰茶嗎？

Can we have another beef curry, please?
我們想再加點一份牛肉咖喱，謝謝。

Could I get a refill, please?
我可以續杯嗎？

bring 帶來	iced tea 冰茶	curry 咖喱
refill 續杯		

9. Check, please.　我要結帳，謝謝。

> pick up the check 買單

吃飽喝足後到了結帳的時刻。關於結帳的英語，我們一般都知道 pay the bill，今天我們來多學一個 Check, please.，這個也是頗為常用、自然的用法。另外，不管你是覺得這次的用餐是 a wonderful meal「一次美食饗宴」還是 a rip-off「一點都不值」，都別忘了給辛苦的服務生來點小費喔！一般而言，美國的 tipping etiquette「小費禮節」是總消費稅前的 15-20%。即便給小費在法律上非必要，但仍代表了我們對餐廳服務生工作的基本尊重。如果服務生的態度或服務真的很糟，我們可以向餐廳的上級投訴，盡量不要不給小費喔！

• 關於「結帳」，你還能這樣說：

Could I have my check, please?
我可以要我的帳單嗎？

Could we have the bill?
我們可以要帳單嗎？

Could we pay, please?
可以幫我們結帳嗎？

bill 帳單

10. This was a lovely dinner.　這次晚餐很愉快。

lovely 令人愉快的

用餐完畢時，不管服務生有沒有問你 Is everything alright? 都不要吝嗇跟他們來一句 This was a lovely dinner. 讓他們覺得辛勤的付出為我們服務是值得的喔！但這句話更多的是出於禮節，接在這句話之後，我們還能說：Have a lovely day! 或 Have a wonderful evening!

・關於「用餐完畢」，你還能這樣說：

Everything was great. Thank you.
這次用餐很愉快，謝謝你！

This was delicious. Thank you.
非常好吃，謝謝你。

I really loved this meal. I had a wonderful time.
我很喜歡這頓飯，真的吃的很開心。

have a wonderful time 過得很開心

1. wine and dine　設宴招待

哈哈：I heard your parents are coming to Taiwan. Where should I wine and dine them?
　　　我聽説妳爸媽要來台灣了，我應該帶他們去哪裡吃頓好料的呢？

Lyla：They will eat anything, except blood…
　　　他們什麼都吃，就是不吃血。

2. go Dutch　各付各的

哈哈：Let me take care of the bill.
　　　我來買單吧！

Lyla：No. Let's go Dutch!
　　　不！我們各付各的吧！

3. It's my treat!　我請客！

哈哈：Do you want to go have some ice cream? It's my treat!
　　　妳想去吃冰淇淋嗎？我請客！

Lyla：Yes! I want to have 10 of them.
　　　好啊！我要吃十個！

4. My eyes are bigger than my stomach.　我想吃得很多，肚子卻裝不下那麼多。

哈哈：Are you full? You're only half way through your meal.
　　　妳吃飽了嗎？妳才吃了一半呢！

Lyla：My eyes are bigger than my stomach.
　　　我就是鯨魚眼小鳥胃！

5. I'm so hungry that I could eat a horse.　我餓到能吃下一匹馬。

哈哈：Finally got a seat in the restaurant.
　　　終於有桌位了！

Lyla：Yeah! I'm so hungry that I could eat a horse now.
　　　是啊！我現在餓到能吃下一匹馬。

第 8 章 哈啦下廚

角色：哈哈（來自台灣）、Lyla（來自美國）

有一種語言學習法叫 Total Physical Response，簡稱 TPR，中文意思是「肢體回應教學法」。簡單來說，TPR 主張透過語言訊息的輸入結合肢體活動能夠促進學習者的語言吸收，讓學習印象更持久。而下廚不正是一個 TPR 教學法典型的活動運用嗎？馬上來學學關於「下廚」的英文對話，然後上廚房親自實驗一下吧！

1. What's your specialty dish?　你的招牌拿手菜是什麼？

specialty　招牌的／ dish　菜

每個人口袋裡至少都有一道拿手菜，即便廚藝再糟的人，多半都還會幾下炒飯、煎蛋、煮泡麵吧！就算做得馬馬虎虎，總要懂得在嘴上吹噓兩句。一起來學學，當別人問你 What's your specialty dish?「你的招牌拿手菜是什麼？」時，可以怎麼回答吧！

• 關於「拿手菜」，你還能這樣說：

My grandma makes the best peach pie.
我外婆做的桃子派是全世界最好吃的。

My Shepherd's pies take some beating.
我做的牧羊人派大概沒有人能超越。

One dish I cook extremely well is clam chowder.
我煮得很好的一道菜是蛤蠣巧達濃湯。

peach　桃子	Shepherd's pie 牧羊人派	take some beating 無人能及
extremely　極度	clam　蛤蜊	chowder　巧達濃湯

2. I always follow the recipe to the letter.　我都是完全按照食譜做的。

recipe　食譜／ to the letter　一字不差

食譜這種東西，有些人是沒有它在廚房就是個廢物（inept in the kitchen），有些人則是僅當參考用。你是屬於哪一種呢？相信很多人都是有一個 from novice to expert「從新手到高手」的過程吧！

- 關於「食譜」，你還能這樣說：

I tweak the recipes every time I make them.

我每次做的時候都會微調一下食譜。

I only use recipes as a guide.

我食譜都只當參考用。

I rarely follow recipes. The process is well-established in my head.

我幾乎不照食譜，因為整個流程都在我腦子裡了。

tweak 微調	guide 指南	rarely 鮮少
process 流程	well-established 完善的	

3. Carefully rinse off the dirt on the asparagus.

仔細地把蘆筍上的塵土沖掉。

rinse 沖洗

在廚房裡，我們經常使用祈使句來下指令，如：Give the cabbage a rinse.「洗一下這個高麗菜。」、whisk your eggs lightly「輕輕把蛋打散」、get the oil round the wok「讓油佈滿整個鍋」等。實地操作後，你會發現：一邊說、一邊做，真的可以記得更牢喔！

- 關於「備料」，你還能這樣說：

I'm gonna quickly chop the chilis.

我來把這些辣椒快速剁碎。

I normally would soak the rice for somewhere around thirteen to fifteen minutes.

我一般會把米浸泡大概十三到十五分鐘。

Let it set for at least thirty minutes for it to take on the flavor of the spices.

靜置至少三十分鐘，讓它能吸收這些香料的味道。

chop 切	chili 辣椒	normally 一般
soak 浸泡	somewhere around 大約	set 靜置
at least 至少	take on 吸收	flavor 味道
spice 香料		

4. First things first. Season the patty.　首先，我們先將肉餅調味一下。

first things first 首先／ season 調味／ patty 肉餅

當我們要開啟一個活動或流程時，我們可以説：first things first，字面意思是「該第一個説的就第一個説」，也就是「首先」啦！另外，我們還可以用 first off、to start with、to begin with 等。終於，開始開火烹飪了！你能看出這些例句當中的句型嗎？別忘了自己嘗試應用一下喔！

• 關於「烹飪流程（一）」，你還能這樣說：

Make sure your grill is piping hot.
記住：你的烤架必須是非常熱的。

Be generous with the garlic.
大蒜盡量放多一點。

After that, just leave it there and let the residual heat do the work.
接下來只要把它放著，讓餘溫繼續把它煎熟就行了。

grill 烤架	piping hot 高溫炙熱的	generous 慷慨的
garlic 大蒜	residual 剩餘的	heat 熱

5. From there, turn it down and let it simmer for twenty minutes.
然後把火關小，讓它悶煮二十分鐘。

from there 接下來／ turn down 調小／ simmer 悶煮

「然後」、「接下來」我們可以用 from there、after that、and now、and then 等衛接詞。烹製過程中，我們也會聽到很多掛在嘴邊的過渡詞，如：Here we go.「來囉！」、OK!「好！」、as that starts to cook「當它開始煮的時候」、

once it's fried off「當它炒乾的時候」等，相信當我們把這些詞句說習慣後，我們的口說一定會聽起來相當不一樣喔！

- 關於「烹飪流程（二）」，你還能這樣說：

So what I will do now is just add water till one third the way up is covered.
我現在要加水到鍋子三分之一的高度。

Just check on the risotto every four or five minutes and give it an occasional stir.
每四到五分鐘檢查一下這個燉飯，偶爾攪拌一下。

I'm gonna bring it up to a boil as quickly as possible.
我現在要盡快把它加溫至沸騰。

till 直到	one third 三分之一	cover 覆蓋
check on 查看	risotto 義大利燉飯	occasional 偶爾的
stir 攪拌	bring to a boil 加溫至沸騰	

6. We start off with 300 grams of rice.　我們先拿三百公克的米。

start off 開始／ gram 公克

關於量的拿捏，很多人也是喜歡 go with his ／ her gut「憑直覺」，畢竟食譜是死的，自己的味蕾和喜好才是活的。這邊我們可以再學一個句式：start off with，如：We start off with 300 grams of rice.「我們先拿三百公克的米。」也可以說成：We take 300 grams of rice to start off with. 而關於「一點點」、「一小撮」，我們可以說：a pinch of，如：a pinch of salt「一小撮鹽」、a twist of，如：a twist of black pepper「一點黑胡椒」、a touch of，如：a touch of olive oil「一點點橄欖油」。

- 關於「量的拿捏」，你還能這樣說：

Get the whole thing in.
整個放下去。

A touch of oil.
一點點油。

The rule of thumb is adding salt according to taste.
一個原則：根據味道來決定加多少鹽。

a touch of 一點點	rule of thumb 準則	salt 鹽
taste 味道		

7. Soy sauce in. 加入醬油。

soy sauce 醬油

俗話說：廚房如戰場，凡事講求快、狠、準，語言當然也需要跟著簡練，因此，Put some soy sauce in. 變成了 Soy sauce in. 或 Soy sauce goes in.「加入醬油。」、Put the rice in. 變成了 Rice in.「把飯加進來。」、Put it onto the fire. 變成了 Onto the fire.「置於火源上方。」注意到了嗎？所有要表達的重點都提到句子最前面了，誰說英語一定得講究語法呢？

- 關於「烹飪快狠準」，你還能這樣說：

Lid on.
蓋上蓋子。

Off with the gas.
關火。

Star anise out.
八角拿出來。

lid 蓋子	off 關掉的	gas 瓦斯
star anise 八角		

8. That's the burger to die for.　這個就是讓你此生無憾的漢堡。

> burger　漢堡／ die for　為……而死

料理完成時，是不是滿意到想昭告天下呢？不管別人覺得好不好吃，自己先誇了再說吧！來看看我們可以用哪些詞句來標榜自己的傑作。要說「色」，我們可以用：beautiful「漂亮的」、delicate「精緻的」、colorful「色彩繽紛的」；要說「香」，我們可以用：aromatic「香的」、fragrant「香的」、smells nice「香的」、smells delicious「聞起來好吃」；要說「味」，我們可以用：delicious「美味的」、tasty「好吃的」amazing「超棒的」、rich「濃郁的」。

• 關於「完成料理」，你還能這樣說：

Boom! Look at those beautiful babies. I'm salivating!
登登！看那些美麗的小可愛！我都流口水了！

We've got a really nice beautifully cooked spaghetti.
我們完成了一道完美的義大利麵。

Bon appétit.
用餐愉快。

boom　用於表示成功、驚喜的語氣詞	salivate　流口水	spaghetti　義大利麵
bon appétit　用餐愉快		

9. I'm a lousy cook.　我的廚藝超爛的。

> lousy　差勁的

如果你的廚藝很差，你可以說：I'm pretty inept in the kitchen.「我在廚房是個廢物。」其中，inept 的意思是「無能的」。另外，你還可以說：Cooking is not my thing.「我不會料理。」或 Cooking is not my strong suit.「料理不是我的強項。」或直接說 I'm a lousy cook.「我的廚藝超爛的」。

• 關於「廚藝拙劣」，你還能這樣說：

It's raw on the inside.
它裡面是生的。

This is obviously overcooked. It's tough.

這個明顯煮過頭了，很硬。

You messed up with the salad. It's too soggy.

你的沙拉搞砸了，太濕了吧！

raw 生的	on the inside 內部	obviously 明顯地
overcooked 煮過頭的	tough 硬的	mess up 搞砸
salad 沙拉	soggy 濕透的	

10. It's all about instinct when it comes to rolling pizza dough.

揉披薩麵團的時候，一切都靠直覺。

instinct 直覺／ roll 揉／ dough 麵團

你做菜的時候會說一堆大道理嗎？如果會，你可能有當主廚的潛質。最後，我們來學學如何闡述自己的烹飪哲學，讓別人沒吃飽先聽飽。

• 關於「烹飪學」，你還能這樣說：

Timing is everything.

掌握時間點非常重要。

You can never rush cooking an onion.

料理洋蔥的時候一定不能急。

Now comes the real trick.

祕訣在這裡。

timing 時機	rush 趕時間	onion 洋蔥
trick 祕訣		

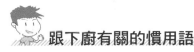

1. to curry favor　討好

哈哈：I'm so sick of Rachel currying favor with Director Jennifer all
the time.
我好看不慣 Rachel 一直討好 Jennifer 主任。

Lyla：If she really enjoys brown-nosing, so be it!
如果她真的喜歡拍馬屁就隨她吧！

2. Too many cooks spoil the broth.　人多手雜。

哈哈：Need some help?
要幫忙嗎？

Lyla：No, we're fine. Too many cooks spoil the broth.
不用，我們可以的，人多手雜。

3. to grill someone　拷問某人

哈哈：How did the meeting go? Did he survive?
開會怎麼樣？他活下來了嗎？

Lyla：Barely! He got grilled about all that stuff.
勉強活下來了，他被拷問了那些事情。

4. to cook up a storm　忙碌地準備大餐

哈哈：What's your mom busy with?
妳媽媽在忙什麼啊？

Lyla：She's been cooking up a storm in the kitchen for Christmas.
她一直在廚房裡準備聖誕大餐。

5. boil down to something　歸結為

哈哈：She told me she quit because she was not happy with the new
salary package she'd been given.
她告訴我她辭職是因為她不滿意公司給她開出的新工資條件。

Lyla：Looks like everything boils down to money at the end of the day.
好像所有事情歸根究底都是因為錢啊！

第９章 哈啦電視

角色：哈哈（來自台灣）、Lyla（來自美國）

電視、追劇讓男女老少都相當瘋狂，兩個人之間多少都能找到曾經看過或同時在追的電視節目，這話題一搭上，往往一聊就能聊上半天。想知道 follow 什麼電視劇、be addicted to、binge-watch 是什麼意思嗎？現在就讓我們一起來哈啦電視學英文吧！

1. What kind of things do you watch?　你都看什麼節目？

> watch　觀看

電視節目大家一般都會想到 program 這個字，其實，問「你看什麼節目」人們一般都說 What kind of things do you watch? 或 What do you watch on TV? 簡單明瞭的開啟話題。

- 關於「詢問看什麼電視節目」，你還能這樣說：

Do you watch much TV?
你常看電視嗎？

What type of TV programs do you watch?
你都看什麼類型的電視節目？

[註]：各類電視節目的英文：drama 戲劇／ sports 體育節目／ sitcom 情境喜劇／
documentary 紀錄片／ soap 連續劇／ cartoon 動畫片／ travel 旅遊節目

Are you watching anything good at the moment?
你現在在看什麼好看的節目嗎？

> program　節目

2. What's that about?　那是關於什麼的節目？

> about　關於……

當對方說了一檔你沒看過的電視節目時，你可以問：What's that about? 意思是「那是關於什麼的？」對方可能簡單的回答：It's about the walking dead.「是關於殭屍的。」或 It's about a love story during World War II.「是關於二戰期間的一段愛情故事。」。如果恰好是自己感興趣的題材，你便可以說：That must be very interesting.「那一定很有趣吧！」或是 I always love...「我一直都很喜歡……」。

- 關於「詢問電視節目相關資訊」，你還能這樣說：

Where's it on?
它在哪裡播？

When is / What time's it on?
它什麼時候／幾點播？

Who's in it?
有誰出演？

> on　上映

3. I'm so into the show.　我好愛這檔節目。

> into　喜歡

要表達「好喜歡……」，我們可以說 I'm so into...。into 的意思是「到裡面」，所以，當某人深陷某事物裡面時，意思就是「深深地喜歡上……」。如果對方說出一檔你剛好也超愛的電視節目，你就可以大喊：Oh my god! I'm so into the show.「天啊！我超愛這檔節目。」

- 關於「喜歡某個節目」，你還能這樣說：

I'm so addicted to the show.
我好迷這個節目。

It's really addictive.
這超讓人上癮。

I can't bear to miss an episode of the series.
我無法錯過這部影集的任何一集。

addicted 成癮的	addictive 令人著迷的	bear to 忍心
miss 錯過	episode 集	series 影集

4. I don't have much interest in those kinds of shows.
我對那種節目沒什麼興趣。

> interest 興趣

當對方聊起一檔自己沒什麼興趣的節目時，與其和他硬聊，不如直接說：I don't have much interest in that.「我對那沒什麼興趣。」另外，我們也可以說：I'm not that interested in...「我對……沒那麼有興趣。」或 I'm not a big fan of...「我不是那麼喜歡……」。

• 關於「不喜歡某個節目」，你還能這樣說：

I got tired of shows that like easily.
那種節目我很容易看膩。

I'm not watching anything with sad endings.
我不想看結尾很悲傷的劇。

I can't bear watching soap operas. They are too melodramatic.
我看肥皂劇會受不了，太狗血了。

get tired of 對……感到厭煩	bear 忍受	ending 結尾
soap opera 連續劇	melodramatic 過分戲劇化的	

5. There's this crime drama I've been watching.

我最近在看這部罪案劇。

crime 犯罪／drama 戲劇

There's this... 這個句型非常適合用來開啟話題。比如：There's this website that helps you learn English. It's very effective.「有一個網站能幫助你學英語，非常有效的。」如果你要向朋友推薦一檔節目，你就可以用上這句：There's this...I've been watching.「我最近一直在看……」。

- 關於「推薦節目」，你還能這樣說：

I've been binge-watching the series recently.
我最近一直在狂追這部劇集。

You should totally check it out.
你一定要去看這部。

Shut up! You've never heard of House? It's like the most popular series these days.
不是吧！你沒聽過豪斯醫生？那是最近最紅的劇集呢！

binge-watch 熱切地看……	recently 最近	check out 查看
hear of 聽說	popular 受歡迎的	these days 最近

6. It's a Netflix production.　它是 Netflix 出品的。

production 製作

目前許多線上影音串流平台也都擁有自己出品、製作或獨家播映的節目，像是 Netflix 出品或獨家播映的節目一般叫做 Netflix originals 或 Netflix productions。另外如果是迪士尼出品的節目就叫 Walt Disney productions。

- 關於「介紹電視節目相關資訊」，你還能這樣說：

It went sensational when it first came out.
它剛播映的時候非常轟動。

It has so many plot twists.

它的劇情轉折非常多。

It went downhill after the second season.

它第二季之後就走下坡了。

go 變得	sensational 轟動的	come out 上映
plot 劇情	twist 轉折	downhill 下坡
season 季度		

7. I don't follow it.　我沒追這部。

> follow 關注

關注或是所謂的「追」某個節目的英文動詞就是 follow。I don't follow it. 就是「我沒在看這個節目」的意思。除了「關注某個節目」，follow 也可以表示「關注某個人的動態」。例如：I follow Jay Chou on Facebook. 意思就是「我關注周杰倫的臉書」。另外，當你聽不懂對方說什麼時，你也可以說 I don't follow. 或 I'm not following.，表示「我聽不懂」。

• 關於「沒關注某節目」，你還能這樣說：

I gave it up a while ago.

我前陣子就不追那部了。

I missed last night's episode.

我錯過昨晚那集了。

Maybe I'll take a look.

我可能會看一下。

give up 放棄	while 一陣子	miss 錯過
episode 集	take a look 看一下	

8. Don't spoil it.　別劇透！

> spoil 毀壞

看電視也有許多不明文的禁忌，劇透、看球賽時說出不吉利的話或支持敵對球隊等，都令人捶胸頓足啊！spoil 在這裡是指「毀壞樂趣」。當對方劇透暴雷時，簡直是毀壞了自己看這部劇的興致，甚至會導致自己再也不想看下去了。此時，你便能先說：Don't spoil it! 堵住對方的嘴，以免造成無可挽回的傷害啊！

• 關於「看電視的禁忌」，你還能這樣說：

Oh, no! You killed all the fun!
噢！不！你壞了一切的興致。

Don't say that! You're gonna jinx it.
別說！等等一語成讖！

Commentator's curse!
球評的詛咒啊！

kill the fun 掃興	jinx 帶來厄運	commentator 球評
curse 詛咒		

9. Stop switching the channels.　別一直轉台！

> switch 轉換／ channel 頻道

每個人看電視都有自己的習性，有些人喜歡不停地換台，看到有趣的節目稍微停留看一下；有些人喜歡把電視機開著卻不看，用聲音來陪伴自己；有些人則喜歡一到廣告時間就轉靜音，抽空去做其他事。其中，switch the channel「轉台」，我們也可以說：change the channels 或 flip the channels。而如果是電視節目主持人要觀眾別轉台，他們通常會說：Stay tuned! We'll be back soon.

• 關於「看電視的個人習慣」，你還能這樣說：

I'm only half watching it. I'm also doing other things.
我只是一半在看而已，我也同時在做其他事。

I only put il on in the background.
我只是把電視開著而已。

I always mute the commercials.
我都會把廣告轉靜音。

half-watching 一半在看	background　背景	mute　靜音
commercial　電視廣告		

10. Stop being a couch potato.　別老是躺在沙發上了。

couch potato　懶骨頭

你會老是癱在沙發上，手上握著洋芋片，眼睛盯著電視螢幕嗎？如果常常這樣，你就是個不折不扣的 couch potato「沙發馬鈴薯」了！愛護眼睛、拒絕臃腫，起來運動一下，告訴自己 Stop being a couch potato!

• 關於「看電視的壞習慣」，你還能這樣說：

Get up and rest your eyes during the ad break.
廣告時間起來讓眼睛休息一下。

We should get up and exercise a little bit during commercials.
我們應該趁廣告時間起身運動一下。

Stop streaming! You need to take a break.
別看了！你需要休息一下。

rest　使休息	ad break　廣告空擋	exercise　運動
stream　串流	take a break　休息一下	

1. The show must go on.　事情還是要繼續下去。

哈哈：I'm so tired. I don't want to do any work.
　　　我好累，不想做任何工作。

Lyla：Come on! You need to get yourself together. The show must go on.
　　　加油！你必須振作起來，事情還是得繼續啊！

2. steal the show　收獲全場的支持和讚美

哈哈：I love Harry's acceptance speech at the Oscars.
　　　我好愛哈利在奧斯卡上的得獎發言。

Lyla：So do I! He totally stole the show.
　　　我也是！他完全獲得滿堂彩。

3. dog and pony show　宣傳性質的作秀活動

哈哈：I really hate to do this demo class every time we have visitors.
　　　我討厭每次我們有訪客來時都要上這種展示課。

Lyla：Bear with it. Just a dog and pony show.
　　　忍一忍吧！只是作秀而已。

4. trial by television　電視公審

哈哈：Media blitz is starting to attack the celebrity really hard.
　　　各種媒體報導已經開始攻訐這位名人了。

Lyla：Seems like he's not going to survive this trial by television this time.
　　　他可能撐不過這次的電視公審了吧。

5. to be in the limelight　成為大眾關注的焦點

哈哈：You're on next. You feeling nervous?
　　　下一個就是妳上場了，緊張嗎？

Lyla：Not at all. I actually quite enjoy being in the limelight.
　　　一點也不，我其實滿享受成為全場焦點的。

第10章 哈啦電影

角色：哈哈（來自台灣）、Lyla（來自美國）

人生如電影，電影如人生。不管是阿宅還是文青，總能聊上幾部電影。而跟外國友人聊電影或相約看電影，更是一種語言、文化交流的大好機會。以下我們就來聊聊哈啦電影的各種場景：從邀約看電影、到電影院買票、談論喜歡或討厭看的電影，到深入談論電影的內容及角色。有時候，來自不同文化的兩個人還可能因為電影的品味相投而成為知己呢！

1. Let's hit the movies tonight. 今晚去看電影吧！

> hit the movies 看電影

hit 是一個很形象的動詞，在字典裡，hit 的意思是「打擊」、「撞擊」。而在口語裡，hit 可以指「去到……」。比如：hit the movies 意思便是「去電影院」、hit the road 表示「上路」、hit the sack 意思則是「上床睡覺」。所以，下次表達「去看電影」，除了 see a movie 之外，也別忘了這個更時尚的說法：hit the movies！

- 關於「邀約看電影」，你還能這樣說：

How about we go see a movie tonight?
今晚去看場電影如何？

Why don't we go to a movie tomorrow?
明天去看場電影如何？

You fancy going for a movie later?
等等要去看電影嗎？

how about 如何	see a movie 看電影	fancy 想要
go for a movie 看電影		

2. What kind of films do you like? 你喜歡看哪種電影？

> film 電影

movie 和 film 都是指「電影」，大致上是可以互換的。然而，在電影專業領域裡工作的人往往更傾向用 film 這個字。另外，根據調查，比起 film，美國人更常說 movie；而在英國，movie 和 film 被使用的比例則相當。另外，what kind of...，我們也可以說：what type of... 或 what sort of，都可以指「什麼種類的……」。

> [註]：電影類型的英文：action 動作片／ comedy 喜劇片／ cartoon 動畫片／ fantasy 奇幻片／ musical 音樂劇／ sci-fi (science-fiction) 科幻片／ rom-com (romantic comedy) 愛情喜劇片

- 關於「電影類型的愛好」，你還能這樣說：

What kind of things, are you into?
你喜歡看什麼類型的電影？

I don't mind watching a horror film.
我不介意看恐怖片。

It doesn't hurt to watch a musical once in a while.
偶爾看一下音樂劇也不錯。

into 喜歡	mind 介意	horror film 恐怖片
it doesn't hurt to... 也無妨	musical 音樂劇	once in a while 偶爾

3. What kind of film is it? 它是什麼類型的片子？

> film 電影

看電影前，很多人喜歡先瞭解一下這部電影的基本資訊，比如：電影類型、上映日期、是原創或改編電影、導演是誰、卡司配置等。若要問電影類型，只要簡單地說：What kind of film is it? 即可。

- 關於「詢問電影的基本資訊」，你還能這樣說：

Is it on in the cinema?
它在電影院上映了嗎？

Is it based on a true story?

它是根據真實事件改編的嗎？

Is that the Woody Allen film?

它是那部伍迪艾倫導的電影嗎？

on 上映	based on 以⋯⋯為基礎

4. It stars Sandra Bullock as a chief editor in a publisher in New York. 它是由珊卓布拉克主演，飾演一名位於紐約的出版社的總編輯。

star 由⋯⋯主演／ chief editor 總編輯／ publisher 出版社

一部電影的卡司或導演往往是決定你是否買票進電影院的關鍵。當談論電影由哪位明星主演時，star 是個很好用的動詞，意思是「由⋯⋯主演」，所以，我們不妨直接把這個句型背起來：It stars...as...「這部電影是由⋯⋯主演⋯⋯角色。」如果是「客串演出」，我們則可以說：Sandra Bullock made a cameo appearance in this movie.「珊卓布拉克在這部電影中客串演出。」

• 關於「介紹電影的資訊」，你還能這樣說：

Ellen Page plays the main character.

艾倫佩姬飾演主角。

It was directed by Steven Spielberg.

它是由史蒂芬史匹柏導演的。

It was dubbed by Jacky Chen.

它是由成龍配音的。

play 出演	main 主要的	character 角色
direct 導演	dub 配音	

5. It was the Oscar-winning film in 2019.

它是 2019 年度奧斯卡獎的得主。

> Oscar 奧斯卡

除了演員、導演之外，電影有沒有得過有份量的獎項，故事場景的設定等，也都是看電影的人感興趣的訊息。尤其是奧斯卡或金馬獎這種含金量高的電影獎，往往能夠為電影的票房及可看性大大加分。如果你想了解一部電影有沒有得過奧斯卡，你可以問：Is it an Oscar-winning film? 而如果是入圍奧斯卡獎的電影，則是：an Oscar-nominated film 或 an Oscar nominee。如果要說某部片入圍了奧斯卡五項大獎，你可以說：It was nominated for five Oscars.

- 關於「介紹電影的更多資訊」，你還能這樣說：

It won several awards at Taipei Film Festival.
它在台北電影節上贏得了許多獎項。

It is set in New York city.
它的故事是設定在紐約。

Most of the story takes place in Bangkok.
大部分的故事都發生在曼谷。

win 贏得	award 獎項	festival 節慶
set 設定	most 大部分的	take place 發生
Bangkok 曼谷		

6. I can't do horror films.　我不敢看恐怖片。

> do 看／ horror film 恐怖片

do 在口語中是一個萬用動詞，在各種語境下有不同的意思解釋。在此處，do 就是「看」的意思。如果要表達「不喜歡看」或「不敢看」某類電影，我們便可以用上 I can't do... 或 I can't stand...。

- 關於「不喜歡的電影類型」，你還能這樣說：

I have a weakness for thrillers, too.
我對驚悚片也沒辦法。

I can't watch anything violent.

我不敢看包含暴力的劇情。

I'm not in the mood for animations today.

我今天不太想看動畫片。

| weakness 弱點 | thriller 驚悚片 | violent 暴力的 |
| animation 動畫片 | in the mood for 有……的心情 | |

7. It got really good reviews. 它的評價非常好。

review 評論

推薦自己喜歡或想看的電影，最常說到的是這部電影的影評極佳，這句話的英文便是：It got really good reviews. 這裡的 reviews 便是「影評」的意思，放到其他情境中也可以指「對某事物的評價」。另外，如果要說一部電影很好笑，英文是 It's hilarious. 如果要說一部電影很具啟發性，英文則是 It's thought-provoking. 如果要說這是你看過史上最棒的電影了，你可以說：It's one of the best films I've ever seen.

• 關於「推薦電影」，你還能這樣說：

It has quite a touching storyline.

它的劇情相當感人。

It had great special effects and incredible action scenes.

它的特效和動作場面都超讚。

The acting was amazing.

演技簡直沒話說。

quite 相當	touching 感人的	storyline 劇情
special effect 特效	incredible 不可思議的	action 動作
scene 場景	acting 演技	

8. It was so predictable.　它的劇情完全都預測的到。

> predictable　可預測的

即便不是人人都能拍電影的年代，也是會出現令人忍不住想吐槽的電影的。有些電影在專業影評裡的確拍得或寫得不夠好，有些也許藝術性太強而曲高和寡，有些則純粹不對你的胃口。總之，關於吐槽電影，有些詞彙我們可以學起來。比如：predictable 便是指「電影劇情俗套」，讓人完全猜測得到；而如果要說電影拍得沒有真實感，或演技生硬，無法說服人，我們可以說：It wasn't believable at all.

• 關於「吐槽電影」，你還能這樣說：

I found it quite boring.
我覺得挺無聊的。

I wasn't impressed.
我覺得還好。

I could barely stay to the end. I wanted to walk out.
我差點坐不到最後，我想直接走出電影院。

impressed　感到印象深刻	barely　幾乎不

9. Have you switched your phone to silent mode?
你把手機調成靜音模式了嗎？

> switch　轉換／silent mode　靜音模式

除了電影本身之外，電影院現場觀眾或同行看電影的夥伴的素質往往也是決定觀影體驗的重要因素。關於在電影院的基本禮儀，最普遍的就是講手機了。對於肆無忌憚地在電影院大講手機的觀眾，有時真的會忍不住施以「白眼之箭」，使他／她「萬箭穿心」！因此，在電影開演前，禮貌性的問問身邊的同伴：Have you switched your phone to silent mode? 免得成為他人白眼之箭的「眾矢之的」。另外，「劇透」也是看電影惡行中的「惡中之惡」，因此，這句也要學起來：Don't spoil it. 或 Don't tell me anything.

- 關於「看電影的習慣」，你還能這樣說：

Would you mind not using your phone, please?
你可以不要使用手機嗎？

Would you mind moving over one seat so my friend and I could sit together?
你可以坐過去一個位置讓我跟我朋友坐一起嗎？

Stop talking! You keep distracting me.
別講話了！你一直干擾我。

distract 使分心

10. Can I get two tickets for Gravity, please?

可以給我兩張地心引力的票嗎？謝謝！

ticket 票

最後，我們來學學在電影院買票或討論時可能會用上的英文吧！買票的基本句型為：Can I get...tickets for..., please?

- 關於「上電影院」，你還能這樣說：

Do you want to have something to snack on while we're watching the movie?
你想買點東西看電影的時候吃嗎？

We have to wait around for an extra hour.
我們必須多等一個小時。

Which theater is the movie showing at?
這部電影在哪廳上映？

| snack on 吃零食 | extra 額外的 | theater 影廳 |

1. popcorn movie　純粹的娛樂片

哈哈：What do you think of Ip Man 4?

妳覺得葉問 4 怎麼樣？

Lyla：I think it's nothing but a popcorn movie.

我覺得就是一部娛樂片。

2. to be a hit / to bomb　很成功／很失敗

哈哈：I think the sequel is better than the first movie.

我覺得第二集比第一集好看。

Lyla：I think the first one was a hit, but the sequel kinda bombed.

我覺得第一集很成功，但第二集拍得很失敗。

3. to be on the edge of my seat　目不轉睛

哈哈：What an exciting movie that was!

好精彩的電影喔！

Lyla：Tell me about it! I was on the edge of my seat the whole time.

就是説啊！我全程眼睛都不敢眨一下。

4. blockbuster　賣座電影

哈哈：I think it could have been a potential blockbuster film.

我覺得它應該可以是一部賣座電影的。

Lyla：Indeed. But time-travel films weren't much of a thing back then.

確實！但當時穿越劇還不太流行。

5. potty humor　低俗幽默

哈哈：It's so hilarious.

這部電影好好笑！

Lyla：I think it went overboard with the potty humor.

我覺得它用了太多低俗的笑話。

第 11 章 哈啦喝酒

角色：哈哈（來自台灣）、Lyla（來自美國）

辛辛苦苦熬過了漫長的一星期，即使累癱也要上酒吧嗨一下啊！尤其對於許多老外來說，上酒吧儼然已成為他們生活中不可或缺的一部份，想了解老外最真實的生活，酒吧絕對是最佳去處！不管是品酒、談心、解悶、療傷、狂歡、交朋友、排遣寂寞，酒吧於日夜之間收集著塵世間各種真實而脆弱的故事。在能夠讀懂這些故事之前，先鍛鍊好酒吧英語，讓自己更得以應對並融入酒吧中的各種語言及文化交流吧！

1. Wanna have a cold one together?　想一起去喝一杯嗎？

a cold one　酒精飲料

邀約別人去喝一杯最簡單的說法就是 Wanna go grab a drink? 其中，drink 在這裡當然就約定俗成地是指「酒」的意思了，所以千萬不要誤會成是要去喝飲料的意思囉！如果是指不含酒精的飲料，我們一般會說 soft drink「軟性飲料」，當然，相對的 hard drink 就是指含酒精的飲料，但這個用法並不普遍。而這句 have a cold one 中的 cold one 也常被用來代指「酒精飲料」或「啤酒」。至於動詞則常搭配 have 或 grab，因此，have a cold one 和 grab a cold one 都可以表達「喝酒」的意思。另外，如果想約朋友上酒吧，我們可以說：Let's go down the boozer. 在這裡，boozer 就是指「喝酒的場所」。

• 關於「邀約喝酒」，你還能這樣說：

Let's go grab a brew.
我們去喝一杯（啤酒）吧！

Let's hit the booze.
一起去大喝一場吧！

Hey, guys! Let's go booze it up!
朋友們！一起去喝一場吧！

grab　抓	brew　啤酒	booze　酒精飲料
booze it up　喝一杯		

2. Can I buy you a drink?　我可以為妳點一杯酒嗎？

> drink　酒

一般而言，除了在速食餐廳裡講 drink 人們會認為是一般的飲料之外，在絕大多數的語境下，drink 都是指含酒精的飲料。所以，當你聽到 Can I buy you a drink? 時，千萬不要不上道地問：What drink? 喔！

[註]：常見的酒的種類：beer 啤酒／ wine 葡萄酒／ liquor 蒸餾酒／ spirit 烈性酒／ cocktail 雞尾酒／ Sake 日本清酒

• 關於「酒吧搭訕」，你還能這樣說：

What do you usually have?
妳通常都喝什麼？

What do you like to drink?
妳想喝什麼？

Make it two.
來兩杯吧！

> have　吃／喝

3. I'm not a big drinker.　我不太喝酒。

> drinker　飲酒者

許多人深受華人社會的勸酒文化之苦，尤其是親戚朋友、公司單位聚餐時，常常能看到各種拚酒、勸酒、起鬨的場面，令人難以招架。雖然這種行為在西方社會比較不常見，但當你和朋友上酒吧時，如果要表明自己不太喝酒，你還是能明確地說：I'm not a big drinker. 通常一般人都能理解的，鮮少出現勸酒的情形。而如果要說自己滴酒不沾，你則可以說：I am a teetotaler.「我完全不喝酒。」意思相當於：I don't drink alcohol.

• 關於「不太喝酒」，你還能這樣說：

I have a low tolerance.
我酒量不好。

I'm a lightweight.
我酒量不好。

One shot and I'm done. I'm such a cheap date.
才喝一杯就醉了，我酒量真是差得可以。

| tolerance 忍受度 | lightweight 酒量差的人 | shot 少量烈酒 |
| done 玩完了的 | cheap date 酒量差的人 | |

4. He is a heavy drinker. 他超能喝。

> heavy drinker 很能喝酒的人

先前我們說到「不太喝酒」的英文是 not a big drinker，然而，如果要說「某人超能喝」，我們卻很少聽到 He is a big drinker. 而是 He is a heavy drinker. 就如同我們稱呼「老菸槍」是 heavy smoker 一樣，都會用 heavy 這個形容詞。另外，用俚語 He is such a lush. 也可以指「他很常跑酒吧。」

• 關於「超能喝」，你還能這樣說：

My boyfriend is an alcoholic.
我男朋友是個酒鬼。

She drinks like a fish.
她很能喝。

He has quite a high tolerance.
他酒量挺好的。

| alcoholic 酒鬼 |

5. Cheers! 乾杯！

cheers 乾杯

cheers 這個不用特別多說了，就是「乾杯」的意思。值得一提的是，在英國，cheers 也可以用來表達：Thanks 或 Bye。比如：Cheers, mate!「謝了！朋友！」以及 Alright, cheers!「好的，再見囉！」可以說，如果一個人在英國待過卻沒有染上 cheers 這個口頭禪的話，可以說他英國白待了。在乾杯時，如果要說「敬…」，我們可以說：To... 比如：To our friendship「敬我們的友誼」、To success「敬成功」或 To life「敬人生」。

- 關於「乾杯」，你還能這樣說：

Bottoms up!
乾杯！

Let's all do a shot!
一起來一杯！

Shall we toast?
來一杯嗎？

bottom 底部	**shot** 少量烈酒	**toast** 舉杯

6. I'm a little tipsy. 我有點微醺了。

tipsy 微醺的

在外喝酒得小心自身安危，如果意識到自己有點喝暈了，可以跟身旁的朋友說：I'm a little tipsy. 這時候朋友便可能問你：Are you sure you can drink more?「你確定你還能喝嗎？」比起 drunk「醉了的」，tipsy 只是「微醺」的意思，也可以說 buzzed。而如果要說自己沒醉、清醒得很，英文則是：I'm stone-cold sober. 當然，大家都知道，真正喝醉的人是不會說自己醉了的。

- 關於「微醺」，你還能這樣說：

You seem to be a little intoxicated.
你好像有點醉了。

I'm a bit merry.

我有點醉了。

I'm mildly inebriated.

我有點微醺。

| seem 似乎 | intoxicated 醉了的 | merry 微醺的 |
| mildly 輕微地 | inebriated 微醺的 | |

7. I was black out drunk last night. 我昨晚喝到斷片了。

black out drunk 不醒人事的酒醉

關於喝醉的英文俚語有上百種，可能得單獨出一本書來介紹吧！其中，最嚴重的「喝到斷片」的英文就是 blackout drunk。blackout 當名詞原本是「斷電」的意思，而 black out 作為動詞片語則是指「昏過去」。因此，black out drunk 就是指「喝到不醒人事」的程度。其他表示「喝醉」的說法，如：hammered、slammed、bombed 是好比「被敲昏」的那種醉；paralytic、legless 是「癱瘓」似的酒醉；而 slaughtered 則是比較誇張地表示有如「被屠殺」的那種醉。

• 關於「喝醉」，你還能這樣說：

You were so wasted.

妳喝得好醉。

I was dead drunk. I can't remember a thing from last night.

我醉死了，想不起昨晚的任何事。

Everybody was under the table.

大家都喝癱了。

| wasted 酒醉的 | dead drunk 醉癱了 |

8. I had a hangover. 我宿醉了。

hangover 宿醉

早上起來口乾舌燥、頭痛欲裂、四肢無力嗎？你宿醉了！也就是傳說中的 hangover。如果作為過去分詞形容詞的形式則是 hungover。口語表達中，我們常用最高級來誇張化事情，所以，如果要說「史上最嚴重的宿醉」，我們可以說 I had the worst hangover this morning.

• 關於「宿醉」，你還能這樣說：

I am hungover from last night.
我昨晚宿醉了。

This morning, I woke up with a pounding headache.
我今天早上醒來的時候頭超痛。

My hangover just won't go away.
我的宿醉就是好不了。

hungover 宿醉的	pounding 陣痛的	headache 頭痛

9. Are you going to be able to drive? 你這樣能開車嗎？

be able to 能夠

「喝酒不開車，開車不喝酒。」酒醉駕車不只是違規，而已是違法行為了。當你開車來的朋友喝酒時，好心提醒一句：Are you going to be able to drive? 如果他回答：I will take a taxi.「我會搭計程車。」或 My friend can drive me.「我朋友會載我。」那便可放心了。「酒醉駕車」的英文是：drunk driving。

• 關於「喝酒不開車」，你還能這樣說：

Are you sure you can drive?
你確定你能開車嗎？

You will be arrested for DUI (driving under influence).
妳酒醉駕車會被逮捕的。

DWI (driving while intoxicated)
酒醉駕車。

arrest 逮捕	influence 影響	intoxicated 酒醉的

10. I'll have a whisky on the rocks. 我要一杯威士忌加冰。

> whisky 威士忌／ on the rocks 加冰塊

如果你不是個很懂酒的人，在和喝酒的朋友 hang out 時可能會像誤闖叢林的小白兔一樣，在喝醉之前就被一堆「成人世界」的喝酒術語迷昏了頭。為了至少能和他們搭上一兩句話，在此羅列幾個身為初學者也該知道的喝酒術語。

- 關於「喝酒的術語」，你還能這樣說：

BYOB (bring your own bottle)
自帶酒水。（用於去別人家喝酒時。）

We're having a liquid lunch.
我們午餐要去喝酒。

I will have a one and one.
給我來杯一對一混酒（酒精飲料對軟性飲料）。

liquid 液體的

 跟喝酒有關的慣用語

1. small beer 不重要的人事物

哈哈：If you're not happy with the arrangement, why don't you tell them?
如果妳不喜歡這個安排，為什麼妳不跟他們提一下呢？

Lyla：I'm small beer to the company's management. Nobody will listen.
我在我公司主管的眼中根本不重要，沒有人會聽的。

2. three sheets to the wind　喝醉站不穩

哈哈：I'm fine. I'm not drunk.

我沒事，我沒醉。

Lyla：Look at you. You are three sheets to the wind.

看看你，你都醉到站不穩了。

3. lose one's bottle　膽怯

哈哈：I wanted to bring it up to my boss, but I lost my bottle at the last minute.

我原本想跟我老闆提的，但最後又怯場了。

Lyla：I should totally bottle your head.

我真該拿瓶子敲你頭。

4. on tap　可立即得到（原指從酒桶裡扭開水龍頭取酒）

哈哈：Hey! The girl in our math class. Do you know if she's dating anyone?

欸！我們數學課上的那個女孩子。妳知道她有沒有男朋友嗎？

Lyla：Ah ha! I happen to have the gossip you want to know on tap.

啊哈！我剛好有你想要知道的八卦。

5. champagne socialist　香檳酒社會主義者（嘴上倡導公平正義卻不身體力行的有錢人）

哈哈：My heart is always with the poor!

我的心永遠和那些窮人在一起！

Lyla：Have you seen the iPhone in your hand? Champagne socialist.

那你手裡的 iPhone 是怎樣？香檳酒社會主義者。

近幾年各國選秀節目盛行，唱歌已成為了全民運動，民間高手各個臥虎藏龍，隨便一抓都能抓到幾副天籟好歌喉。又說音樂是世界共通的語言，一首歌能勾起許多人同個時代的回憶，同時又是來自各地的人了解並學習另一個語言和文化的窗口。本章節我們就來聊聊和唱歌相關的日常口語對話吧！

1. Let's go karaoke singing.　一起去唱 KTV 吧！

karaoke　卡拉 OK

可別以為 KTV 只有在亞洲地區風行喔！許多歐美人下了班之後，除了上酒吧喝酒之外，唱 K 也是他們解壓娛樂的首選。跟亞洲不同的是，歐美比較少有獨立的 karaoke place，而通常是設置在餐廳或酒吧裡的。在英國，有許多 KTV 是設置在中式餐館裡，外面是用餐的地方，裡面就是吃飽飯後飆歌的 KTV。但 KTV 這個詞通常只有在亞洲會使用，全名是 karaoke television，在英文中，通常就直接叫 karaoke。當你和朋友相約唱 K 時，可以用上這個句型：go karaoke singing，這其實就是大家很熟悉的 go shopping、go swimming 的句型喔！

• 關於「相約 K 歌」，你還能這樣說：

You wanna go do karaoke?
你想去唱 KTV 嗎？

We should get together for karaoke sometime.
我們找時間一起去唱 KTV。

We're going to karaoke Friday.
我們星期五要去唱 KTV。

karaoke　唱 KTV

2. This song is called Hero by Mariah Carey.

這首歌是瑪莉雅凱莉的「英雄」。

> called 被叫做／ by 由……主唱

聽到一首超好聽的歌，我們通常會問：這首歌是誰唱的？在英文中，我們就可以用上 by 這個介系詞，表示「被……所唱」，比如：This song is by Maroon 5.「這首歌是魔力紅唱的。」

• 關於「談論歌手」，你還能這樣說：

Who's this song by?
這首歌是誰唱的？

The song sounds odd. Who's the singer?
這首歌聽起來好奇怪，是誰唱的？

The song is written and sung by Linkin Park. They're the greatest band ever to exist.
這是歌是由聯合公園創作並主唱的，他們是有史以來最棒的樂團。

sound 聽起來	odd 奇怪的	exist 存在

3. What's the song called?　這首歌叫什麼？

> call 稱作

聽到一首歌超好聽時，我們通常也會忍不住問：這首歌叫什麼？英文就是用被動語態 be called。在演唱會中，歌手在介紹歌曲時，也常常會說：This song is called...。另外，要問這首是什麼歌，我們也可以說：What song is this?

• 關於「談論歌名」，你還能這樣說：

This song sounds beautiful. What's the title?
這首歌好好聽！歌名叫什麼？

What's the name of the song that goes …?
這首歌的名字是什麼？它是這樣唱的……。

They call it Free Falling.
這首歌叫「自由下落」。

title 歌名

4. It goes like this, "Hey Jude, don't make it bad…"
它是這樣唱的：Hey Jude, don't make it bad…。

go 說；唱

要表達：「這首歌是這樣唱的」時，如果你是說：The song sings like… 那你就錯囉！正確的說法是：The song goes like...。這裡的 go 就是表示「講起來是……」或「唱起來是……」的意思，後面可接某首歌或某句話的內容。另外，如：as the saying goes 意思就是「俗話說的好」。

• 關於「這歌怎麼唱」，你還能這樣說：

I can't remember the exact lyrics but it went something like…
我不記得確切的歌詞，但好像是……

I can only sing the chorus.
我只會唱副歌。

Sorry. I mixed up the lyrics.
抱歉，我歌詞唱錯了。

exact 確切的	lyrics 歌詞	chorus 副歌
mix up 搞混		

5. It is one of the greatest hits this year.　它是今年最紅的歌之一。

hit 火紅的事物

如果你想推薦一首當下的最夯金曲，hit 是一個很好用的字，它表示「當下非常火紅的事物」。而 hit 這個字本身在本章節的語境下即可表示「極受歡迎的歌曲」，也可以說成：hit song 或 hit single。另外，現在很多素人會將自己的音

樂創作或翻唱作品上傳到網路平台上，被人瘋狂轉載而爆紅，而爆紅的英文就是 go viral，亦即如病毒般地蔓延，如：The song went viral with tens of millions of views on Youtube.「這首歌一夕爆紅，在 Youtube 平台上累積了幾千萬的觀看次數。」

- 關於「火紅的歌」，你還能這樣說：

It's a hot song.
這首歌超紅。

The song is number one on the charts.
這首是排行榜第一名的歌。

It's always on my playlist.
這首歌一直在我的播放清單裡。

chart 排行榜	playlist 播放清單

6. I can't get the song out of my head.　我的腦子裡一直是這首歌。

get...out of　將……去除

相信大家都有被一首歌洗腦的經驗吧，一旦中了這種 earworm「耳蟲」的毒，那當下滿腦子都得充滿那首歌的旋律，還會情不自禁地哼唱出來，這種時候你便能說：I can't get the song out of my head.

- 關於「洗腦歌」，你還能這樣說：

The song just got stuck in my head.
這首歌一直在我的腦海中迴響。

The tune from the movie keeps playing in my head.
那部電影裡的那首歌一直在我腦中不停播放。

This song is an earworm.
這首歌太洗腦了。

stuck 困住的	tune 曲調	earworm 洗腦歌

7. You've got a great voice.　你的歌聲好棒。

> have got　有

歌聲的英文是 voice，而稱讚別人的歌聲很棒，我們可以說：You have a great voice. 或 You've got a great voice.。一般而言，have 比較正式，have got 比較口語，並且 have 常和主詞縮寫，在非常隨性的口語語境中，have got 還可以再簡化成 got，如：You got a great voice.。此外，稱讚歌聲優美，我們還能說：You've got a voice of an angel.「你擁有天使般的歌聲。」而要稱讚某人的歌聲極富情感，我們可以說：You really sang your heart out.。

• 關於「歌聲動人」，你還能這樣說：

Wow! That was beautiful.
哇！好好聽喔！

I didn't know you could sing like that.
我不知道你唱歌那麼好聽。

I can't get enough of your voice.
我好喜歡你的歌聲啊！

> can't get enough of　聽不膩

8. You should totally audition for American Idol.
你完全應該去參加美國偶像啊！

> audition　試鏡

每個時期似乎都有一檔屬於當代的選秀節目，許多歌壇的天王天后都是從選秀節目發跡的，這似乎告訴著我們：有才華的人只要有勇氣去嘗試，是金子都總會發光的。因此，你和妳都可能是發掘大明星的星探！當你遇到一把明星級的好聲音時，拍拍他／她的肩膀，眼神誠懇地說：You should totally audition for… 說不準他／她就因為你的一句話，成為下一個張惠妹或蕭敬騰呢！

• 關於「吹捧未來之星」，你還能這樣說：

You should try out for Britains Got Talent.
你應該去參加英國達人秀的。

You could totally be a pop star.
你簡直可以去當歌星了。

You can be the next John Mayer.
你能成為下一個約翰梅爾。

try out 嘗試	pop 流行的

9. I wish I could sing. 但願我會唱歌。

wish 但願

羨慕別人的好歌喉，感慨但願自己會唱歌就好了，這時你可以用上這個虛擬式的結構：I wish I could...。在這句當中，wish 後面引出的子句表示一種虛擬的情況，動詞需用過去簡單式。

- 關於「不會唱歌」，你還能這樣說：

I can't carry a tune.
我五音不全。

I can't sing that high.
我唱不上去。

Singing is not my thing.
我不愛唱歌。

tune 曲調

10. Who told you you could do this?　誰告訴你你可以當歌星的？

> tell　告訴

還記得藉由擔任美國偶像評審而成名的 Simon Cowell 經典的一句話嗎：I don't mean to be rude, but...「我無意冒犯，但……。」這種尖酸刻薄的毒舌評審雖然常常引發爭議，但也使得選秀節目看頭十足，常常讓觀眾又氣憤又愛看。接下來，我們就來學學幾句毒舌金句吧！記得：僅限朋友之間開玩笑使用！

- 關於「毒舌評審金句」，你還能這樣說：

You should try something else.
你該改行試試了。

Singing is not for everybody.
不是人人都能唱歌的。

You have neither the look nor the voice to make it in this industry.
你既沒臉蛋，也沒歌聲，還想在這行業混？

industry　行業	look　長相	make it　成功
neither…nor　既不……也不		

 跟唱歌有關的慣用語：

1. If you sing before breakfast, you'll cry before night.
別高興過早。

哈哈：I think our product is gonna be a big success.
　　　我覺得我們的產品一定會很成功。

Lyla：Well, if you sing before breakfast, you'll cry before night. Let's wait until everything is completed.
　　　別高興過早，等到一切都完成了再下定論吧！

2. until the fat lady sings　事情還沒結束前別下定論

哈哈：We are down by twenty points. There's no way we can win.
　　　我們落後了二十分，根本不可能贏了。

Lyla：Come on! It's not over until the fat lady sings.
　　　加油啊！比賽還沒結束前別放棄。

3. sing for one's supper　付出勞力換取報酬

哈哈：Can he stay here for dinner?
　　　他可以留下來吃晚餐嗎？

Lyla：Yes, hecan, but he needs to sing for his supper by doing the
　　　dishes for me.
　　　可以，但他得付出勞力，幫我洗所有的碗盤。

4. call the tune　身為決策者、負責人

哈哈：No. I don't want to do the dishes.
　　　不要，我不想洗碗。

Lyla：You should listen to me. I call the tune here.
　　　你應該聽我的！這裡我說的算。

5. sing a different tune　改變立場

哈哈：Why are you singing a different tune now? You never like your
　　　boss.
　　　為什麼妳突然改變立場了？妳不是不喜歡妳老闆嗎？

Lyla：Well, he made me his partner. How can I not like him?
　　　嗯⋯⋯他升我為合夥人了啊！我怎麼能不喜歡他呢？

第13章　哈啦派對

角色：哈哈（來自台灣）、Lyla（來自美國）

歐美人是著了名的愛開派對，各種名目都能拿來開派對，最常見的便是節慶相關的 Christmas party「聖誕派對」、Halloween party「萬聖節派對」，吃相關的 dinner party「晚餐派對」、barbecue party「烤肉派對」，工作相關的 launch party「產品發佈派對」、after party「慶功派對」和各種主題相關的 retro party「復古派對」、Caribbean-themed party「加勒比海主題派對」等。因此，跟著老外一起跑趴絕對是一個認識朋友、鍛鍊英文的好方法。在開始跑趴之前，我們先來練習在派對上會使用到的各種英語對話吧！

1. We're having a party at Jim's. Are you up for it?

我們要在 Jim 家辦派對，你要來嗎？

have a party 舉辦派對／ up for sth. 有興趣做某事

西方人非常喜歡在家裡開派對，有的派對很盛大，有的派對就只是幾位親朋好友到家裡簡單地吃個飯，喝個小酒。這種在自家舉辦的派對叫 house party。一般的 house party 分兩種：一種是主人準備好所有的食物和酒水，參加的人只要人到了就好；另一種則是每組參加的客人必須準備一道自製的菜餚或點心帶到派對主人家，這種就叫 potluck party。有些派對則是酒水不由主辦人提供，而是由客人自帶，這種我們叫 BYOB（bring your own bottle）或（bring your own booze）。

當我們要邀請別人參加 house party 時，我們可以說：We're having a party at ○○○'s. 其中，舉辦派對除了用 have a party 之外，throw a party 也是很常聽到的用法。另外，本句中的 Jim's 表示 Jim's place「Jim 的家」，是老外講話時很常使用的省略法。

• 關於「邀約參加派對」，你還能這樣說：

I'm having a dinner party in my new place. I'd love it if you could come.
我要在我新家辦一次晚餐派對，希望你能來參加。

My friend is throwing a backyard barbecue party. Are you coming?
我朋友在辦一場庭院烤肉趴，你想去嗎？

Let's get down tonight.

今晚一起去派對吧！

[註]：10 種派對類型的英文：birthday party 生日派對／ dinner party 晚餐派對／ cocktail party 雞尾酒派對／ garden party 花園派對／ housewarming party 喬遷派對／ welcome party 歡迎派對／ farewell party 送別派對／ after party 慶功派對／ pool party 泳池派對／ costume party 化裝舞會

| place 住處 | throw 舉辦 | backyard 後院 |
| barbecue 烤肉 | get down 去派對跳舞狂歡 | |

2. Thanks for having me over. I'm so happy to be here.

謝謝你邀我來，來到這裡我超開心的。

> have sb. over 邀請某人作客

受邀參加派對的第一個場景當然是到達派對現場了。當我們剛抵達別人家時，首先當然要來一句「感謝邀請」囉！這句的英文就是 Thanks for having me over. 或 Thanks for having me. 這裡的 have 便是「邀請」的意思。接著，我們可以開始表達自己的心情，比如：I'm so happy to be here. 或 I'm so excited to be here. 或是稱讚一下主人的房子很漂亮：Your house is so beautiful. 或主人的衣服很美：Your dress is beautiful. I love it. It's gorgeous. 等等的。總之，就是用各種讚嘆和稱讚來表達你的興奮和榮幸之情。

• 關於「派對主人和客人的交流」，你還能這樣說：

Thanks for inviting me.

謝謝你邀我來。

Thanks for having us. What a beautiful house!

謝謝你邀請我們來。好美的房子啊！

I'm so glad that you guys could come. Please make yourselves at home.

好開心你們能夠來，請不要客氣喔。

| invite 邀請 | glad 開心的 | make yourself at home 別客氣 |

3. Hi. I'm Ryan. Nice to meet you. 　嗨！我是 Ryan，很高興認識你。

> **nice to meet you** 很高興認識你

派對是一個結交新朋友和鍛鍊英語交際能力非常好的場合。在派對上，我們需學會如何簡短有力的介紹自己，或介紹朋友給另外的朋友認識。這時，不論是真心的交友還是客套的往來，語言都得盡量保持簡單、大方、得體。自我介紹完後，通常都會接個 Nice to meet you.、Nice meeting you.、Good to meet you. 或 Pleased to meet you. 等。

- 關於「派對上的人際交流」，你還能這樣說：

Ryan, this is Elissa. Elissa, this is Ryan.
Ryan，這位是 Elissa，Elissa，這位是 Ryan。

Hi. I don't think we've met.
嗨，我們之前沒見過吧。

I guess you guys have spoken earlier.
我想你們之前應該談過了。

guess 猜想	**earlier** 先前

4. How do you know Alisha? 　你怎麼認識 Alisha 的？

> **know** 認識

在派對上，朋友把你介紹給了新朋友認識，這時，該怎麼破冰呢？最好的話題當然就是你們的共同好友囉！你可以問：How do you know... ？「你怎麼認識……的？」如果是工作認識的，我們可以說：We work together.；如果是同學，我們可以說：We went to high school together. 或 We were classmates.

- 關於「怎麼認識的」，你還能這樣說：

Alisha and I go way back.
我和 Alisha 認識很久了。

We went to university together.
我們是大學同學。

We met through friends.
我們是朋友介紹認識的。

go way back 認識許久	university 大學	through 透過

5. What brings you to Taiwan? 你怎麼會來台灣？

> bring 帶來

接著，我們來聊聊在派對上能聊些什麼吧！聊完共同好友後，想要更深入地認識對方，我們不妨從「當下所在的城市」聊起。這裡當然不是要你聊城市建設或市長滿意度這種話題，而是對方和這座城市之間的關係，從而由這個點來引出對方更多的故事。比如：What brings you to...?「你怎麼會來……？」就是一個相當好引起話題的問句喔！不信的話下次不妨試試！

- 關於「派對話題：地方」，你還能這樣說：

  You come from here?
  你是本地人嗎？

  Do you live in the city?
  你住市區嗎？

  How do you find Taipei?
  你覺得台北怎麼樣？

> find 認為

6. How did you get into architecture? 你怎麼踏進建築這一行的？

> get into 進入／architecture 建築

派對雖然是比較輕鬆隨意的場合，但和初次見面的朋友聊天還是盡量避免交淺言深，建議還是圍繞著一些周邊的話題，比如：工作。接著，再適當地根據對方的反應來決定是否可以繼續深聊。聊工作時，我們可以問對方：How did you get into...?「你怎麼進入……這一行的？」這也是一句相當好展開話題的問句，相信也能引出一段 long story 喔！

- 關於「派對話題：工作」，你還能這樣說：

How did you become an engineer?

你怎麼成為工程師的？

How is it at your company?

你公司怎麼樣啊？

Do you work or are you a student?

你在工作了還是還在讀書？

engineer 工程師

7. You having fun?　你還好嗎？

have fun 玩得開心

在派對上總有這個情境：在 mingle「交際」一陣過後，鏡頭拉回到吧台旁或某個安靜的角落，對話從眾人間的喧囂變成了兩人世界，這時最常出現的開場對話便是：You having fun? 或 Having fun? 意思大概是：「還好嗎？」、「玩得怎麼樣？」這類簡單的問句可以成功地將人聲鼎沸的氣氛轉變成兩人獨處的模式，從而開啟深入的兩人對談。

- 關於「派對搭訕語言」，你還能這樣說：

Hey. There you are. You having a good time?

嘿！你在這啊！玩得還開心嗎？

It's freezing inside. You good?

裡面超冷的，你還好嗎？

What were you guys talking about a second ago?

你們剛剛在聊什麼啊？

have a good time 玩得開心	burning hot 炎熱的

8. You guys wanna stick around and play some poker?
你們想留下來玩撲克牌嗎？

> stick around 待著／poker 撲克牌

派對上，為了活絡氣氛，認識朋友，人們經常會玩一些互動小遊戲，比較經典的比如有：poker「撲克牌」、darts「射飛鏢」、truth or dare「真心話大冒險」、King's Cup「國王杯」……等。再者，不外乎就是無盡的喝酒及攀談。現在我們就來學學在參與這些活動時會說到的常用句子吧！

- 關於「派對活動」，你還能這樣說：

I'm gonna take a dip in the pool.
我去泳池裡玩一下。

I'd better go and mingle.
我要去走走聊聊。

I'm gonna buy a round.
我來買一輪酒。

| take a dip 去游泳 | pool 泳池 | had better 最好 |
| mingle 交際 | | |

9. Thanks for telling me about your school. We should talk more.
謝謝你告訴我你學校的事，我們找時間再多聊聊。

> tell 告訴

在派對上，不論你是相談甚歡，或是遇到了話不投機三句都嫌多的人，總有你得結束對話，離開現場的時刻。這時我們該如何明確又不失禮貌地結束對話呢？當然，我們可以直接說：I gotta go.「我得先走了。」或 I'm heading out.「我要離開了。」但更友善的方式是：向對方表達此次對話的收穫和愉悅的心情。比如：Thanks for telling me about...「謝謝你告訴我……的事。」或 I really like your...story.「我覺得你的……故事超棒的。」接著，表達想與對方保持聯繫，我們可以說：We should talk more.「我們再找時間聊聊。」讓對方覺得自己還有

意猶未盡的感覺，但由於某些原因不得不先離開。如此一來，便能讓整段對話的結束不會顯得唐突而無禮。

- 關於「結束對話」，你還能這樣說：

It's been really nice talking to you. You've got some good stories.
和你聊天很開心，你的故事超棒的！

We should get together sometime.
我們應該再聚聚。

I'd like to stay in touch. Can I have your number?
我想和你保持聯繫，我可以加一下你的電話號碼嗎？

have got 有	get together 相聚	stay in touch 保持聯繫

10. Thanks again for having me. I really had a good time.
謝謝你邀我來，我玩得很開心。

> have 邀請／have a good time 玩得開心

離開派對前，別忘了和主人道別，並再次感謝他／她的邀請喔！這時，我們可以說：Thanks again for having me. I really had a good time. 你也可以提一下這場派對令你印象深刻的地方，比如：I absolutely love the chocolate fondue.「我超愛你們的巧克力噴泉的。」讓派對主人感受到你的稱讚是真心而實際的。

- 關於「離開派對」，你還能這樣說：

I gotta go. It's been really nice meeting you.
我得走了，真的很高興認識你。

I'm sorry to have to leave early. I hope to see you again soon.
不好意思我得先離開了，希望能很快再見到你。

I'm sorry to stop you, but I'm afraid I've got to go home now.
不好意思打斷你，我現在得先回家了。

afraid 恐怕

1. party animal　派對動物

哈哈：What do you think of Jeffery? You think he's good husband material?

妳覺得 Jeffery 怎麼樣？妳覺得他會是個好老公嗎？

Lyla：Absolutely not. He's too much of a party animal.

絕對不是，他就是一個派對咖。

2. party pooper　派對上掃興的人

哈哈：You think it's a good idea to invite Bob over?

妳覺得邀請 Bob 來怎麼樣？

Lyla：You don't want to do it. He's totally a party pooper.

千萬不要，他超級掃興的。

3. crash the party　亂入派對

哈哈：Let's crash the party. It'll be fun.

我們去亂入人家的派對吧！一定很好玩！

Lyla：You think that's a good idea? Well…Let's go!

這樣好嗎？嗯……那走吧！

4. the party is over　歡樂的時間過去了

哈哈：I heard Director Samuel is leaving.

我聽說 Samuel 主任要走了。

Lyla：Yeah. And Rosa is taking over his job. I guess the party is over.

對啊！而且 Rosa 要接替他的工作，我看歡樂的時光是過去了。

5. the life of the party　聚會的靈魂人物

哈哈：Who should I invite to the party?

我該邀誰來參加派對呢？

Lyla：Definitely Janet! She's the life of the party. She literally knows everyone in town.

當然是 Janet！她可是派對的靈魂呢！她幾乎認識鎮上的所有人。

第 14 章 哈啦八卦

角色：哈哈（來自台灣）、Lyla（來自美國）

人的本性都是愛聽八卦的，一群朋友不管熟不熟，聚在一起時就愛聊八卦。聊八卦不僅能拉近彼此間的距離，還能創造出一種團體歸屬感，甚至成為一種社交手段、人際籌碼，然而當自己淪為八卦的受害者時，又會對八卦心生畏懼、敬而遠之。現在，我們就一起用英文來認識這讓人又愛又恨的八卦吧！

1. You won't believe what happened. 你一定不會相信發生了什麼。

believe 相信／ happen 發生

相信你一定聽過這些開場白。聊八卦時，一定要加上這幾句，讓聽者的耳朵先豎起來！比如：I have to tell you about this.「我一定要跟你說這件事。」記得把這幾句練熟，講的時候語速快一點，才會有 feel 喔！

• 關於「八卦開場白」，你還能這樣說：

Oh my God! You know Mr. Lee is leaving.
天啊！李老師要離開了！

Guess what!? I saw Fiona with a new guy I've never met before.
猜猜看發生了什麼？我看到 Fiona 跟一個我從沒見過的男生在一起。

Have you heard about Peter quitting his job?
你聽說 Peter 辭職的事了嗎？

hear about 聽說	quit 辭去

2. This is just between us. 這件事我只跟你講。

between 在⋯⋯之間

Promise you won't tell?「你保證不說嗎？」This is just between us.「這事我只跟你講。」I shouldn't tell anyone, but I have to tell you this!「我不該跟任何人說的，但我必須告訴你！」熟悉嗎？這些就是八卦如何一傳十、十傳百的！所以下次當你要跟信任的人透露祕密時，think again!

- 關於「透露祕密」，你還能這樣說：

Don't tell anyone.

別告訴別人。

I can't say.

我不能說。

I wish I could tell you more, but my lips are sealed.

我也想告訴你多一點，但我不能說。

lips 嘴唇	seal 密封

3. No way!　不是吧！

> no way 不可能

當個稱職的吃瓜人，就是要學會這幾種戲劇化的反應啊！其中，No way! 除了能表示「不允許」之外，還有「不敢置信」的意思。記得說的時候語氣要誇張、眼睛要瞪大喔！

- 關於「聽八卦的反應」，你還能這樣說：

Shut up!

不是吧！

I can't believe it.

不敢相信。

That's mental!

太瘋狂了！

mental 瘋狂的

4. Are you still in touch with any of our old colleagues?

你還有在跟我們的舊同事聯繫嗎？

> in touch with　與……聯繫／colleague　同事

詢問某某的最新消息，或開始挖某個人的料，我們可以從這幾句開始。Are you still in touch with...?「你還有在跟……聯繫嗎？」回答時可以說：Yeah! He just messaged me the other day.「有啊！他前幾天才剛發訊息給我。」或 No! I haven't talked to her for a long time.「沒有！我很久沒跟她聊了。」

• 關於「與誰聯繫」，你還能這樣說：

Do you still talk to Celine?
你還有在跟 Celine 聯繫嗎？

Have you heard from Joseph lately?
你最近有聽到 Joseph 的消息嗎？

I don't have him on Facebook.
我沒有他的臉書。

> **hear from**　得到……的消息

5. When did they start seeing each other?　他們什麼時候開始交往的？

> see each other　交往

八卦時最常聊的話題非感情莫屬了。關於誰和誰在一起，我們常用的動詞除了 date 之外，還可以說 see。如：Are you seeing anybody?「你在和誰交往嗎？」、When did they start seeing each other?「他們什麼時候開始交往的？」值得一提的是，date 和 see 都是指結婚前的交往，而如果要問一對已婚的夫婦從何時開始交往的，我們會用 be together，如：How long have you been together?「你們在一起多久了？」

• 關於「八卦交往」，你還能這樣說：

Hey! Do you know Brian's been dating Rachel?
嘿！你知道 Brian 在跟 Rachel 交往嗎？

There's something going on between them.
他們兩個好像怪怪的。

They've been together for a month. Don't you know that?
他們已經在一起一個月了，你不知道嗎？

date 交往	together 在一起

6. So he dumped her?　所以他甩了她嗎？

> dump 甩

「甩」的英文是 dump 或 ditch。I dumped my boyfriend. 意思就是「我把我的男朋友甩了。」另外，在口語中，so 是一個很常用的發語詞，幾乎可以用在任何句子的開始，如：So they didn't break up?「所以他們沒分手？」、So what's going on?「所以怎麼了？」、So is it true that she cheated on him?「所以她出軌的事是真的嗎？」

- 關於「八卦分手」，你還能這樣說：

That's history.
那已經是過去的事了。

I heard they broke up already.
我聽說他們已經分手了。

I thought they split up.
我以為他們分手了。

history 歷史	break up 分手	thought 以為
split up 分手		

7. I think they would make a perfect match.　我覺得他們挺登對的。

> make　成為／match　一對

英文裡有一個詞是 juicy gossip「有料的八卦」，形容的太貼切了！可不是嗎？一段感情中，從曖昧、交往、熱戀、不合到分手，只要有 juice 的地方都會被八卦群眾一一榨乾，這其中的酸甜苦辣，包含抵禦槍林彈雨般的流言蜚語的過程，到頭來也只有當事人最明白啊！話說回來，我們先來學學一段感情中的各種階段，我們可以怎麼八卦！

- 關於「八卦感情狀態」，你還能這樣說：

How many times were you in love?
你談過幾次戀愛？

I heard she's just moved in with Mark.
我聽說她剛跟 Mark 開始同居。

He's off the market.
他脫單了。

in love　戀愛	off the market　脫離單身

8. He's a player.　他是個花心男。

> player　玩咖

無論是網路上或現實生活中，群起攻訐各種渣男壞女的情景想必大家都不陌生吧！在這過程中，彷彿大家都站到了一個陣營，心都凝聚在了一起，罵完之後彷彿正義得到了伸張，壞人得到了制裁。我想這應該就是聊八卦之所以解壓的原因吧！

- 關於「八卦渣男渣女」，你還能這樣說：

So she cheated on him?
所以是她劈腿嗎？

He's a two-timing bastard.
他是個劈腿的渣男。

That doesn't surprise me. He's very flirtatious.

我不驚訝，他很喜歡跟別人打情罵俏。

cheat 欺騙	two-timing 劈腿的	bastard 壞蛋
surprise 使驚訝	flirtatious 輕挑的	

9. They just don't get along with each other. 他們就是不合。

get along with 與……相處融洽

除了感情之外，職場也是一個滋生八卦的大溫床！從各種陣營、小團體、上司、下屬、跳槽、升遷等千百樣種錯綜複雜的風雲劇場，都直接成為了大家配飯、配酒的一碟碟八卦小菜，上班的壓力想必就是靠這些八卦排解的吧！

• 關於「八卦職場」，你還能這樣說：

The other day I was talking with Elissa and she said she got promoted.

前幾天我在跟 Elissa 聊天，她跟我說她升遷了。

So they picked Lucy eventually. I bet Malia wasn't too happy with that.

他們最後選了 Lucy，我想 Malia 一定很不爽吧。

I ran into my new boss and she's super nice.

我遇到我的新老闆，她人超好的！

the other day 幾天前	promote 升遷	pick 選
eventually 最後	run into 巧遇	

10. I don't mind other people's business. 我對別人的事沒興趣。

> mind 介意／ business 事情

教完了大家如何八卦，最後，還是呼籲各位，面對八卦謠言，還是要以客觀、理性的心態去面對，偶爾八卦幾句，調劑身心即可！不要過度地依賴八卦作為人際交往的手段。下次，當你被問到某某八卦時，最明哲保身的作法還是説聲：

I don't mind people's business.「我對別人的事沒興趣。」

* 關於「如何應對八卦」，你還能這樣説：

What other people think is their business, not yours.
別人怎麼想是他們的事，跟你無關。

I couldn't care less. Not interested.
我完全不在意，沒興趣！

Stop being nosey!
別八卦了！

business 事情	couldn't care less 完全不在意	interested 感興趣的
nosey 愛探聽他人私事的		

 跟八卦有關的慣用語

1. juicy gossip 有料的八卦

哈哈：What do you do on your girls' night out?
你們姊妹淘之夜都在做什麼？

Lyla：Talking about all that juicy gossip! That's what we do to decompress.
當然是聊八卦啊！那是我們解壓的方式。

2. stick my nose into people's business　探聽別人的私事

哈哈：Why do you always stick your nose into people's business?
　　　妳幹麻老是探聽別人的私事？

Lyla：I don't. I'm just concerned.
　　　我沒有啊！我只是關心一下。

3. dish the dirt　爆前任情人的黑料

哈哈：Anna dished the dirt on her ex.
　　　Anna 爆了她前男友的黑料。

Lyla：That's horrible. I didn't know she would be a backstabber.
　　　太可怕了！我不知道她是這種會耍陰招的人。

4. be a blabbermouth　大嘴巴

哈哈：Don't tell her anything. She always takes a bit of information and makes it bigger.
　　　別告訴她任何事，她老是捕風捉影，又誇大其詞。

Lyla：I know. She's a blabbermouth.
　　　我知道！她是個大嘴巴。

5. hear it through the grapevine　從小道消息得知

哈哈：How do you know they're gonna cancel our travel benefits?
　　　妳怎麼知道他們要取消我們的旅遊福利？

Lyla：It's not official. I just heard it through the grapevine.
　　　還不確定，只是個小道消息。

第 15 章　哈啦偶像

角色：哈哈（來自台灣）、Lyla（來自美國）

偶像對於一個人的英文能力的影響是很深遠的，這一點都不誇張！很多追逐王力宏、陶喆或其他西洋歌手、演員的迷弟迷妹們都練就了一口好英語呢！即使追的不是英語為母語的偶像，在國際應援會的社群裡，與其他地區的迷友交流，或在網路上與心儀的偶像互動，確實成為了許多人學英語的動力。今天不管你是哈日、哈韓還是哈洋的各種迷、各種粉，都一起來學學如何用英文哈啦偶像吧！

1. My greatest influence was Michael Jackson.

影響我最深的人是 Michael Jackson。

> great 大的／ influence 影響

關於「偶像」，我們通常會用的字有：idol、influence 和 inspiration，後兩者都有「啟發」的意思。比如：Haruki Murakami is my biggest inspiration.「村上春樹是影響我最深的人。」反過來説，「迷」、「粉」的英文則是 fan，而 die-hard fan 意思就是「死忠粉絲」、「鐵粉」，如：I'm a die-hard Linkin Park fan.「我是一個死忠的聯合公園粉絲。」

• 關於「我的偶像」，你還能這樣説：

An-Lee is the director who inspires me the most.
李安是啟發我最深的一位導演。

I suppose my idol would be Kobe Bryant. I've been a Kobe fan since 2004.
我的偶像是 Kobe Bryant 吧！我從 2004 年開始就一直是 Kobe 的粉絲。

I've got so many influences. As far as popular music is concerned, there'd be people like Katy Perry, Adele and Lady Gaga.
我有很多偶像。在流行音樂方面，像是 Katy Perry、Adele、Lady Gaga 都是我的偶像。

director 導演	inspire 啟發	idol 偶像
inspiration 啟發		

2. Don't you know Whitney Houston? She was big back in the 80s. 你不知道 Whitney Houston 嗎？她在八零年代超紅的。

> big 當紅的

要說某某偶像「很紅」，我們通常會用 famous、well-known、a household name 等，但其實我們還能用一個更簡單、更道地的說法，那就是 big。比如：He was big in the 90s.「他在九零年代超紅的。」但如果別人說了某某名人，我們卻還是黑人問號時，我們可以說：That doesn't ring a bell.「我沒印象。」

• 關於「聽過某某偶像」，你還能這樣說：

You know her? The one from the Youtube video?
你知道她嗎？ Youtube 影片裡的那個？

He's only famous locally. You've probably never heard of him.
他只在當地比較有名，你可能沒有聽過他。

He goes by Rock Giant.
他以「搖滾巨人」這個稱號聞名。

locally 在本地	probably 可能	hear of 聽說
go by 以……名號為人所知		

3. His main claim to fame is his role as Jack in Titanic.
他成名主要是因為演了鐵達尼號的 Jack 的角色。

> main 主要的／ claim to fame 成名原因／ role 角色

「成名」的英文有：become famous、become known、rise to fame 等。而「因……成名」我們可以說：He became famous for... 或直接用片語 claim to fame「成名原因」：His claim to fame is...「他因為……成名。」

• 關於「偶像如何成名」，你還能這樣說：

He became known for designing the suspension bridge.
他設計了這座吊橋之後就成名了。

She became an international worldwide sensation after her video went viral on Youtube.

她的影片在 Youtube 上爆紅之後，她成為了一個國際名人。

She was spotted by a talent agent in New York City.

她在紐約被星探發掘。

known 有名的	design 設計	suspension bridge 吊橋
international 國際的	worldwide 全世界的	sensation 轟動
go viral 爆紅	spot 發現	talent agent 星探

4. BTS means so so much to me.　BTS 對我來說好重要。

mean 具有意義

偶像之所以能成為偶像，一開始可能是因為他們的作品或演出，但更重要的往往是他們對我們的人生帶來了什麼影響，促使我們做出了什麼重要的決定。在表達偶像對我們的重要性時，我們可以說：...means so much to me.「……對我來說好重要。」或誇張一點的 ...means the world to me「……是我的世界。」

• 關於「偶像對我來說」，你還能這樣說：

They gave me a lot of confidence that I didn't have before.

他們讓我變得比以前更有自信。

They have helped me through so much in my life.

他們在我人生中幫助過我很多。

They're kinda part of my life.

他們像是我生命的一部份。

confidence 信心

5. He's one of the best blues players on the planet, if not the best. 他是地球上最棒的藍調演奏家之一。

> blues 藍調／ player 演奏家／ planet 星球／ if not the best 即使不是第一

想要大力推銷自己的偶像，我們可以用這個句型：...is one of the best..., if not the best.「……是最棒的……之一，即使不是最棒的。」可以表達一種高度推崇，同時避免過於武斷的語氣。

• 關於「推崇偶像」，你還能這樣說：

I just love him and his voice makes me crazy.
我就是愛他，他的歌聲令我瘋狂。

He's one-of-a-kind. He's undefeated. He's the truth.
他是獨一無二，永不言敗的，他是真理。

I feel like what makes him attracted to people is that he always has a strong passion for everything he loves and would go to the extreme to try to get it.
我覺得他會那麼吸引人的原因是，他總是對他所熱愛的一切事物抱持熱情，並且會竭盡所能地去達成。

voice 歌聲	one-of-a-kind 獨一無二的	undefeated 不敗的
passion 熱情	go to the extreme 竭盡所能	

6. He was playing parts in small variety shows before he got a role in a blockbuster movie. 他在得到那部賣座電影中的角色之前都在小型綜藝節目中扮演各種角色。

> play 扮演／ part 角色／ variety show 綜藝節目／ role 角色／ blockbuster movie 暢銷電影

身為一個明星的粉絲，應該要能如數家珍地講出明星職業生涯的各種工作和發展吧！這邊我們可以運用過去進行式來表示某某明星先前某段時間一直在從事

的事，而使用現在進行式則可以表示明星現在一直在從事的事，如：He was playing parts in small variety shows.「他當時在小型綜藝節目裡演各種角色。」He's shooting another film.「他現在在拍另一部片子。」

• 關於「偶像的工作」，你還能這樣說：

She also dabbles in directing.
她也涉足導演工作。

He was classically trained, so he's very good at blending R & B with classical music.
他之前是接受古典音樂訓練的，所以他很擅長把節奏藍調和古典樂結合在一起。

They decided to go on an indefinite hiatus after winning six Golden Melody Awards in Taiwan.
他們在贏得六項台灣金曲獎獎項後決定無限期單飛不解散。

dabble in 涉獵	direct 導演	classically 古典地
train 訓練	blend 融合	classical music 古典音樂
go on a hiatus 單飛不解散	indefinite 無限期的	award 獎項

7. He starred in a science fiction thriller in 2007.
他於 2007 年在一部科幻驚悚片中演出。

star 主演／ science fiction 科幻片／ thriller 驚悚片

介紹偶像時，經常會提到他們參與過的作品，比如電影、專輯等。其中，「在電影中演出」我們可以說：play a role in...；「主演」可以用動詞 star；「拍片」可以說 shoot a film。

• 關於「偶像的作品」，你還能這樣說：

This is his most personal album.
這是他最個人化的專輯。

His latest film received mixed reviews but I thought it was pretty good.

他最新的電影得到了兩極的評價，但我覺得還不錯。

In his latest album, he moved away from the country music that characterized his early records and started experimenting with blues and rock music.

在他的最新專輯中，他摒棄了他早期專輯較具代表性的鄉村音樂風格，而開始實驗藍調和搖滾樂。

personal 個人性的	mixed 好壞參半的	review 評價
album 專輯	move away from 摒棄	country music 鄉村音樂
characterize 展現特色	record 唱片	experiment 實驗
blues 藍調	rock 搖滾	

8. Lee has been nominated for nine Academy Awards.

李已經被提名過九次奧斯卡獎。

nominate 提名／Academy Award 奧斯卡獎

偶像得了什麼獎、創了什麼紀錄，常常讓身為粉絲的自己覺得彷彿是自己辦到了似的。無論如何，這種與有榮焉的心理要怎麼驕傲地和別人炫耀呢？一般我們會運用現在完成式，表示偶像到目前為止達到了什麼成就或紀錄，但如果是已故的偶像，那就得用過去簡單式了。

• 關於「偶像的成就」，你還能這樣說：

If I'm not mistaken, he's sold some fifteen million albums.

如果我沒記錯的話，他的專輯已經賣了大約一千五百萬張。

They're the first Taiwanese band to perform at Madison Square Garden.

他們是第一組在麥迪遜花園廣場表演的樂團。

He won hundreds of awards, more than any other popular music artist.

他獲得過上百個獎項，比其他任何流行音樂藝人都多。

mistaken 錯誤的	some 大約	perform 表演
artist 藝人		

9. Is she dating Brad Pitt?　她現在在跟 Brad Pitt 交往嗎？

> date 交往

八卦人人愛，尤其是明星的八卦，常常成為朋友之間茶餘飯後的配茶點心。其中，最常被拿來八卦的應該是明星的感情狀態了。比如：「某某在跟某某交往嗎？」英文就是用 Is...dating...?；而「某某跟某某分手了嗎？」則是 Did...break up with...?；「他們又復合了嗎？」我們可以說：Did they get back together?

• 關於「偶像的八卦」，你還能這樣說：

Has she had plastic surgery?

她有整型嗎？

He has a history of cheating.

他之前曾對感情不忠。

There's a lot of misinformation on the web about him.

網路上有很多關於他的不實傳言。

plastic surgery 整形手術	cheat 欺騙	misinformation 錯誤資訊
web 網路		

10. He's a super famous artist, but he does not put on airs.

他是個超有名的藝人，但他沒什麼架子。

> artist 藝術家／put on airs 擺架子

很多明星患有大頭症、擺架子，很多則是以禮貌、親民著稱，關於這些用語，在英文中又是如何表達的呢？看完之後你會發現，英文的說法也是很形象的喔！

- 關於「偶包架子」，你還能這樣說：

They are so down-to-earth.
他們很平易近人。

Jennifer enjoys being a regular person and doesn't take herself too seriously.
Jennifer 喜歡當個平凡人，也不會自視甚高。

She has a reputation for being out of touch.
她是個著名的與世事脫節的明星。

down-to-earth 平易近人的	regular 普通的	take oneself seriously 自以為是
reputation 名聲	out of touch 與……脫節	

 跟偶像有關的慣用語

1. get a big head 大頭症

哈哈：I love Angeline so much. She's super famous now but she doesn't get a big head about it.
　　　我超愛 Angeline 的，她即使現在已經超有名了，卻一點大頭症都沒有。

Lyla：Yeah! I heard she's even nice to paparazzi.
　　　對啊！我聽說她甚至對狗仔都很好。

2. jack of all trades, master of none　樣樣通，樣樣鬆

哈哈：My idol is Popu-boys. I think they're so versatile.
　　　我的偶像是 Popu-boys，我覺得他們真是多才多藝。

Lyla：Jack of all trades, master of none.
　　　還不都樣樣通，樣樣鬆。

3. one trick pony　只會一種把戲的人

哈哈：I never thought he could make it till today.
　　　我從來沒想過他可以撐到今天。

Lyla：Me either. One trick pony. Mostly by luck I guess.
　　　我也是，就只會一種把戲，都是靠運氣的吧我想！

4. be in the limelight　出風頭

哈哈：He mentioned he didn't enjoy being in the limelight.
　　　他説過他不喜歡成為鎂光燈的焦點。

Lyla：That's something only famous people say.
　　　這種話只有已經出名的人才會説。

5. has-been　過氣的名人

哈哈：I bet she did that just to get people's attention.
　　　我賭她那樣只是為了得到大家的關注罷了。

Lyla：Nobody would care. She's just a has-been TV star.
　　　沒有人會在乎的，她只不過是個過氣的電視明星而已。

第16章 哈啦星座

角色：哈哈（來自台灣）、Lyla（來自美國）

I'm a zodiac sign expert. I can tell what your sign is.

Okay! What's mine?

You're a bit bossy, so you must be a Leo.

No, I'm not.

Well...since you're stingy all the time, you must be a Taurus.

Wrong again! Who says I'm stingy!!!

Now I got it. Your temper is so bad. You ARE an Aries for sure.

Fine... you're right.

星座算是個信者恆信，不信者恆不信的話題。但當星座迷遇上另一個星座迷時，那簡直可以聊上三天三夜都不夠呢！不管你信不信星座，喜不喜歡星座，它都算是一個交際時很常遇到的話題，因此，本章節我們就一起來學學如何用英語聊星座吧！

1. What is your zodiac sign?　你是什麼星座的？

> zodiac　黃道帶

What's your zodiac sign? 或 What's your sign? 是一句很老套的搭訕話術，意思是「你是什麼星座的？」其中，zodiac sign 也可以說成 the sign of the zodiac，意思是「黃道帶上的標誌」，也就是俗稱的「星座」。另外，星座還可以說成：astrological sign 或 star sign，但這兩者較不常用。

[註]：十二星座的英文：Aries 白羊座／Taurus 金牛座／Gemini 雙子座／Cancer 巨蟹座／Leo 獅子座／Virgo 處女座／Libra 天秤座／Scorpio 天蠍座／Sagittarius 射手座／Capricorn 摩羯座／Aquarius 水瓶座／Pisces 雙魚座

• 關於「了解對方星座」，你還能這樣說：

I'm a Virgo.
我是處女座的。

He's a Libra man.
他是個天秤男。

I was born under the Sagittarius sign.
我是射手座的。

Virgo　處女座	Libra　天秤座	be born under　生於
Sagittarius　射手座	sign　星座	

2. Taurus are born between April 20 and May 20.
金牛座是四月二十到五月二十之間。

> Taurus 金牛座／ be born 出生／ between…and… 介於……之間

由於不是人人都熟悉星座，因此，當我們聊到星座時，甚至會遇到自己是什麼星座都不知道的人，這時，我們就能用上這個句型來幫對方科普一下星座的日期範圍。

- 關於「星座日期」，你還能這樣說：

Aquarius season takes place from January 21 to February 19.
水瓶座是從一月二十一日到二月十九日。

She was born in Leo season.
她是在獅子座的月份出生的。

My birthday falls under the Capricorn sign.
我的生日是在摩羯座期間。

Aquarius 水瓶座	season 季	take place 發生
Leo 獅子座	fall under 時間於	Capricorn 摩羯座
sign 星座		

3. I absolutely believe in astrology. 我超相信星座的。

> absolutely 絕對／ astrology 星座

聊到星座時，如果你剛好是個星座迷，這時你就可以興奮地大喊：I absolutely believe in astrology.「我超相信星座的。」或 I am so into astrology.「我超愛星座的。」absolutely 有「絕對」、「超級」、「非常」的意思。而 believe in 的意思是「相信某事物的存在」。

- 關於「相信星座」，你還能這樣說：

I read my horoscope every single morning.
我每天早上都會看我的星座運勢。

I live and breathe astrology.
我是個星座迷。

This is so accurate.
這超準的。

| horoscope 星占 | live and breathe 痴迷 | accurate 準確的 |

4. I don't believe in astrology. 我不信星座。

believe in 相信

有些人痴迷星座，有些人則對星座嗤之以鼻，認為星座是不科學的無稽之談。如果你是個不相信星座的人，你可以說：I don't believe in astrology.「我不信星座。」記住不要說成：I don't believe astrology. believe 是表示「相信某事或某人說的話為真」；而 believe in 則是指「相信某事物的存在」。在此語境中，我們應該使用後者的 believe in. 另外，「不信星座」，我們也可以說：I don't relate to it.

• 關於「不信星座」，你還能這樣說：

I'm not into astrology.
我對星座沒興趣。

I'm not opposed to astrology, but I just don't want to learn about it.
我不反對星座，但我就是不想去了解。

I just don't see myself believing in astrology. There's no logic to this thing.
我不相信星座，這種東西一點邏輯都沒有。

| into 喜歡 | be opposed to 反對 | logic 邏輯 |

5. You must be a Gemini. 你一定是雙子座的。

> must 肯定

相信星座的人很喜歡根據對方的言行舉止來猜測對方的星座。如果你覺得對方像極了某某座的人，你便可以說：You must be...「你一定是……座的。」本句中的 must 是表示「推測」的情態助動詞。

- 關於「猜星座」，你還能這樣說：

I'm gonna say you're a Scorpio.
我覺得你是天蠍座。

You, I'm gonna go with Aquarius.
你，我覺得應該是水瓶座的。

What makes me an Aries to you?
為什麼你覺得我是白羊座？

> **go with** 猜測

6. Sagittarians have a reputation for being very romantic.
射手座以非常浪漫聞名。

> reputation 名聲／ romantic 浪漫的

當你知道對方的星座後，我們可以先聊聊那個星座的優點。這時，我們可以學一些固定的句型，再把各種形容詞套入即可。比如：...have a reputation for being...「……座以……聞名。」

- 關於「星座的優點」，你還能這樣說：

Leos are born leaders.
獅子座是天生的領導者。

Taurus people are resilient as hell.
金牛座的人韌性超強。

Pisces are good as their word.

雙魚座非常守信用。

born 天生的	resilient 堅韌的	as hell 極端地
good as one's word 守信用		

7. Leos are notorious for being self-centered.

獅子座是出了名的自我中心。

notorious 惡名昭彰的／ self-centered 自我中心

各種星座也有各種惡名昭彰的缺點，雖然很多是刻板印象，但也不失為一個聊天的好素材。同樣地，我們也可以套用幾個固定的句型：...are notorious for...、...are known to be...、...are often seen as...、...can be... 等。

• 關於「星座的缺點」，你還能這樣說：

Libras are known to be indecisive and delusional.

天秤座是出了名的優柔寡斷和異想天開。

Scorpios are often seen as reckless, impulsive and proud.

天蠍座通常被認為是很魯莽、衝動並驕傲的。

Virgos can be stubborn and overconfident.

處女座有時很固執且過度自信。

indecisive 優柔寡斷	delusional 愛妄想的	reckless 魯莽的
impulsive 衝動的	proud 驕傲的	stubborn 固執的
overconfident 過度自信的		

8. Sagittarians are said to be active go getters.

射手座被認為是積極的行動派。

active 積極的／ go getter 行動力強的人

除了優缺點外，每個星座還有它們獨特而鮮明的性格，而這些都能成為聊星座時的話題。如果你想維持你星座專家的形象，不妨再多學以下幾句，幫助你繼續絮絮叨叨這個話題。

• 關於「星座的性格」，你還能這樣說：

Capricorns are considered to be patient and warm-hearted.
摩羯座被認為是非常有耐心且暖心的。

Virgos are known for being good at reading people. However, they can also be very moody.
眾所皆知處女座非常會看人，但同時也非常情緒化。

Cancers have a crazy side that only comes out around close friends.
巨蟹座瘋狂的一面只會在熟人面前展現出來。

consider 認為	patient 有耐心的	warm-hearted 暖心的
be known for 以……著名	be good at 擅長	moody 情緒化的
side 面向	come out 顯露	close 親近的

9. Aries is a perfect match for Gemini. 白羊座和雙子座是完美的一對。

match 配對的人

聊星座時，怎麼能錯過「配對」compatibility 這個話題呢！？某某星座和某某星座是天生佳偶或是天生怨偶，不管是星座愛好者還是吃瓜群眾都相當感興趣呢！聊配對時，我們可以用上這個句型：...is a perfect match for...「……座和……座是完美的一對。」

- 關於「星座配對」，你還能這樣說：

Gemini and Aquarius could make a dynamic duo.
雙子座和水瓶座有很大的機會能湊成一對佳偶。

Logical Scorpio may struggle with intuitive Pisces.
講究邏輯的天蠍座可能會與直覺性強的雙魚座處不來。

Outspoken Aries can be put off by Libra's passive aggressive tendencies.
有話直說的白羊座可能會受不了天秤座執拗消極的個性。

dynamic 有力量的	duo 一對	logical 邏輯好的
struggle 遇到困難	outspoken 直言的	put off 使感到厭煩
passive 消極的	aggressive 攻擊的	tendency 傾向

10. Today, your career will reach a decisive moment.

今天你的職涯會到達一個決定性的時刻。

career 職涯／ reach 到達／ decisive 決定性的

最後，如果朋友圈裡剛好有位星座專家，那可能不免俗地大家會需要聽聽各種星座的本週或本月運勢。如果那位星座專家剛巧是你，那這幾句你必須得學！如果那位星座專家是別人，那這幾句學起來我們至少能聽得懂。不管你相不相信，喜不喜歡，至少能當作茶餘飯後的聊天消遣。最重要的是要 Follow your own path. Live your own life.

- 關於「星座運勢」，你還能這樣說：

The horoscope says you should be more careful this month.
星占說你這個月要當心點。

Your expenses will shoot through the roof if you don't pay careful attention to your finances.
如果你不謹慎對待你的財務，你的支出將會爆表。

You will find yourself at an advantageous point in your field.
你將會在你的專業領域佔據優勢。

horoscope 星占	careful 小心的	expense 支出
shoot through the roof 暴增	pay attention to 注意	finance 財務
advantageous 優勢的	field 領域	

 跟星座有關的慣用語：

1. tough cookie 頑強、意志堅定的人

哈哈：You think Vivian is able to make it this time? She's in such a tough situation.
妳覺得 Vivian 這次能成功嗎？她現在遭遇的麻煩可大的呢！

Lyla：Don't worry about her. She's a tough cookie.
不用擔心她，她可頑強了。

2. have a quick temper 性子急

哈哈：I heard the new director has a quick temper. She must be an Aries.
我聽說新來的主管脾氣很急躁，她一定是個白羊座。

Lyla：Everybody is an Aries to you cause you always can find a way to get on their nerves.
對你來說全世界的人都是白羊座，因為你總是可以把大家都惹毛。

3. social butterfly 社交能手

哈哈：Mick is such a social butterfly. He must be a Sagittarian.
Mick 超社交的，他肯定是射手座的。

Lyla：Like you know him. He's a Taurus.
你根本就不了解他，他明明是個金牛座。

4. as straight as an arrow　生性正直

Lyla：Do you think I can trust Eric?

你覺得我可以信任 Eric 嗎？

哈哈：Of course you can. He's as straight as an arrow.

當然可以啦！他是個正直的人。

5. as stubborn as a mule　生性固執

哈哈：Your friend, Susan, is as stubborn as a mule. No matter what I say, she just wouldn't listen.

妳的朋友 Susan 真是固執地像一頭牛。不管我説什麼，她就是不聽。

Lyla：Let me talk to her. She'll do whatever I say.

讓我和她談談，我説什麼她都會照做的。

第17章 哈啦美妝

角色：哈哈（來自台灣）、Lyla（來自美國）

一般講到化妝品，我們都會提到兩個英文字，一個是 cosmetics，另一個是 makeup。cosmetics 的範圍較廣，包含從頭到腳的化妝品、保養品、清潔用品和各種裝束，而 makeup 通常只是針對臉部的化妝品，但兩者通常都可以在商店的同一區找到。今天，不管你是男是女，喜歡化妝或痛恨化妝，倘若你在生活中聊到化妝品時，不想當個邊緣人，就一起來學學如何簡單地哈啦美妝吧！

1. Girls buy more makeup than they'd like to admit.

女孩們都不願意承認她們超愛買化妝品。

> makeup 化妝品／ admit 承認

如果說養寵物燒錢的話，養化妝品絕對也是不遑多讓。參觀女孩子的化妝品櫃，絕對堪比參觀古董收藏家的展示櫃，除了不理解為何同樣的產品可以有五、六罐之外，瓶身上的楔形文字也永遠在腦中形成不了意義。覺得不誇張嗎？如果是，那你讀讀這些句子，肯定也會覺得不能同意更多！

• 關於「女孩的第二生命」，你還能這樣說：

I can't live without these products.
我沒有這些化妝品活不下去。

She's a makeup addict.
她化妝成癮了。

I use makeup almost every day.
我幾乎每天都會化妝。

product 產品	addict 成癮者

2. The first thing you wanna do before you start doing your makeup is making sure your skin is clean.

妳上妝前的第一步一定要確定妳的皮膚是乾淨的。

> makeup 化妝

如果一枚直男不能理解和網紅甜品拍照，還花大半天時間修圖的樂趣，那他一定也很常吐槽那位在化妝鏡前摸一個多小時女友。雖然你不想知道她們到底這一個多小時做了些什麼，但還是一起來勉強了解一下，為自己開啟新世界的大門吧！其中，我們可以注意到，化妝用的動詞我們可以用 do、use 和 wear 等。

[註]：常見化妝品的英文：primer 妝前乳／ foundation 粉底／ pressed powder 粉餅／ concealer 遮瑕膏／ blush 腮紅／ eye shadow 眼影／ eyeliner 眼線筆／ mascara 睫毛膏／ brow pencil 眉筆／ lipstick 口紅

• 關於「化妝步驟（一）」，你還能這樣說：

You always apply the moisturizer first.
妳一定要先擦保濕霜。

You wanna give it a second, wait till it sets in your skin.
你必須等它被吸收進去。

I usually start out by applying a couple of dots right there.
我通常一開始會先擦上幾個小點。

apply 塗抹	moisturizer 保濕霜	set in 吸收進去
start out 開始	apply 塗抹	a couple of 幾個
dot 點		

3. I'd just dab that in little specks over my face.

我一般會一點一點輕輕點在臉上。

> dab 輕點／ speck 斑點

上妝時，我們會用到很多不同的動詞，如：apply「塗抹」、dab「輕點」、tap「輕拍」、pop「塗上」、rub「揉」等。最好的記法就是使用肢體反應學習法，一邊跟著做，一邊讀出這些動詞，至於男生的話，嗯……。

- 關於「化妝步驟（二）」，你還能這樣說：

I'd normally bring it down a little further into the region where I want to highlight it.
我一般會把它刷下來到我想強調的區域。

Underneath my eyes is the region I take very seriously.
眼下是我很著重的部位。

That's pretty much it. I'm good to go.
這樣就差不多完成了，我準備好了。

normally 一般	region 區域	highlight 強調
underneath 在下方	take seriously 注重	good to go 準備好

4. It comes in 40 shades and it has six shade families.

它有四十個色號，六個色系。

come in 有／ shade 色號／ shade family 色系

come in 意思是「有……種類」，如：It comes in various shades.「它有好幾種色號。」另外，介紹化妝品是什麼品牌，我們可以用 from 來表示，如：This is from Dior.「這是 Dior 出的。」

- 關於「介紹化妝品」，你還能這樣說：

I got it in the shade 11.
我買的是 11 色號的。

This is from Maybelline. It's their brow pencil.
這隻是媚比琳的眉筆。

That one is richer and more hydrating.
那款比較厚，也比較保濕。

brow pencil 眉筆	rich 厚重的	hydrating 保濕的

5. It is going to make your eyes look more lifted.
它會讓你的眼睛看起來更往上提。

lift 提起

介紹化妝品效果時，我們一樣可以善用我們已會的動詞，像是：make「使……」，如：make it look brighter「讓它看起來更亮」、cancel out「蓋掉」，如：Peach orange cancels out dark blue.「桃子色可以蓋掉深藍色。」、bring「帶來」和 give「給」，如：It brings dimension to your face.「它讓你的臉看起來更立體。」。

• 關於「化妝品效果」，你還能這樣說：

Light orange cancels out the color blue.
淺橘色能蓋住藍色。

It brings a dewy finish to your eyes.
它能在最後修飾妳的眼睛，給妳一種清透感。

It can give your face certain dimension.
它可以讓你的臉看起來更立體。

| cancel out 抵消 | bring 帶來 | dewy 清透的 |
| finish 修飾 | certain 特定的 | dimension 維度 |

6. I've been loving using this magic eye cream.
我最近很喜歡用這款眼霜。

eye cream 眼霜

I've been loving to...「我最近很喜歡……。」是一個推薦東西時超級好用的句型，如：I've been loving to use this contour.「我最近很喜歡用這款修容粉。」另外，go-to 也是一個很常聽到的形容詞，表示「必用的」或「必找的」，如：This is my go-to mascara.「這款是我必用的睫毛膏。」也可以用來形容人，如：Daniel is my go-to guy when it comes to drinking.「Daniel 是我喝酒時必找的人。」

• 關於「推薦化妝品」，你還能這樣說：

Every girl needs this in their makeup kit. Nothing beats this one.
每個女孩子的化妝包裡都需要這個，沒有比這個更好的了。

This is definitely my go-to foundation for every day.
這是我每天必用的粉底。

It is so lightweight feeling. It's my best friend.
它超輕薄的，它是我的好朋友。

makeup kit 化妝包	beat 打敗	definitely 絕對
go-to 必用的	foundation 粉底	lightweight 輕薄的

7. My foundation wears off my face so quickly. 　我的粉底掉得好快。

> foundation 粉底／ wear off 脫落

wear off 有「磨損」、「剝落」的意思，這邊表示「脫妝」，另外，我們也可以說：rub off、slip off、melt off、slide out of place 或 separate。如果是「浮粉」，我們可以說 getting cakey；如果是「卡粉」，則是 creasing，如：How do you stop your foundation from creasing?「妳怎麼防止粉底卡粉的？」

• 關於「化妝品缺點」，你還能這樣說：

It always gets cakey.
它老是會浮粉。

It feels super sticky and thick.
它超黏、超厚重的。

It would start balling up in the creases of my face.
它會在我臉部皺紋的地方開始糊成一片。

cakey 糕狀的	sticky 黏的	thick 厚重的
ball up 糊成一片	crease 摺痕	

8. I'm pretty insecure about how I look without makeup.

我對自己不化妝的樣子很沒有安全感。

> insecure 不安全的

所謂的「女為悅己者容」，在英文口語中有一個說法是：I want to look my best for someone I'm into.「我想要在我喜歡的人面前看起來是完美的。」然而，其實有很多男生是偏好素顏路線的，他們追求的是那種自然、清新的感覺，但即便如此，很多女生素顏時還是覺得非常赤裸、不自在，而這種女生對於「素顏」being barefaced 會有什麼表示呢？

- 關於「素顏」，你還能這樣說：

I normally don't go to work barefaced because I don't want people to think I don't care to be at this thing.
我一般都不會素顏去上班，因為我不想讓別人覺得我不重視我的工作。

I'm not wearing makeup. You can see the blue veins popping through underneath the eyes.
我沒化妝，你可以看到眼睛下面的藍色血管很明顯。

If I don't have makeup on, it will look like I'm unprofessional.
如果我沒化妝，我會看起來很不專業。

barefaced 素顏的	vein 靜脈	pop 突出
unprofessional 不專業的		

9. My skin is more on the oily side.　我的皮膚比較偏油性。

> oily 油的／ on the...side 偏……的

人的皮膚類型可分為 normal「中性」、oily「油性」、dry「乾性」和 combination「混和性」四種。而常見的皮膚狀況有 sensitive skin「敏感肌」、dehydrated「皮膚脫水」、rash「疹子」和 acne「痘痘」等。如果要說「我的皮膚比較偏油性」，我們可以說：My skin is more on the oily side. 其中，on the...side 表示「偏……」，又如：She's more on the fat side.「她有點偏胖。」

- 關於「皮膚狀況」，你還能這樣說：

You have oily skin.
你是油性皮膚的。

Your skin is dehydrated.
你的皮膚缺水了。

Her skin is almost poreless.
她的皮膚幾乎沒有毛孔。

oily 油性的	dehydrated 缺水的	poreless 無毛孔的

10. When you wash your face, try to cleanse it for about two minutes to let the cleanser do its job.
你洗臉的時候，大約要洗兩分鐘才能讓洗面乳發揮作用。

cleanse 清洗／cleanser 洗面乳／do its job 發揮作用

不管化不化妝，想要有美美的臉蛋最重要的還是臉部保養的功夫啦！一旦擁有良好的皮膚基底，即使不上妝自己還是能由衷地散發自信的！

- 關於「皮膚保養」，你還能這樣說：

Put it on your fingertips and do a circular motion to gently rub it into your skin.
取一點在指尖上，做畫圓的動作把它擦進妳的皮膚裡。

My T-zone is especially oily, so I make sure it is exfoliated.
我的 T 字部位特別油，所以我會特別對這個部位去角質。

If you don't cleanse it off properly, it can clog up your pores.
如果你沒有好好清潔的話，它會堵住你的毛孔。

fingertip 指尖	circular 圓的	motion 動作
gently 輕柔地	rub 揉	T-zone T 字部位
especially 特別地	exfoliate 去角質	properly 適當地
clog up 堵住	pore 毛孔	

1. put one's face on　化妝

哈哈：How much longer do you need? I'm starving!
　　　妳還要多久啊？我快餓死了！

Lyla：I still need to put my face on. You can just go ahead. I'll meet you at the restaurant.
　　　我還要化妝欸！你可以先去，我直接去餐廳找你。

2. as pretty as a picture　美得像畫一樣

哈哈：Wow! I can't believe my eyes. You're as pretty as a picture.
　　　哇！我真不敢相信我的眼睛，妳今天美得跟畫一樣。

Lyla：I just feel so awkward with the stuff on my face.
　　　我臉上化那麼多東西好不習慣！

3. Beauty is in the eye of the beholder.　情人眼裡出西施。

哈哈：I've never understood why Ted is so crazy about Sara. She's ugly!
　　　我始終搞不懂為什麼 Ted 那麼喜歡 Sara，她那麼醜！

Lyla：Don't say that! Beauty is in the eye of the beholder.
　　　別這麼説！情人眼裡出西施啊！

4. Beauty is more than skin deep.　美貌不過一層皮。

哈哈：I just can't seem to find a girlfriend. I'm too short, not good looking enough.
　　　我感覺我根本找不到女朋友，我那麼矮，長得又不夠好看。

Lyla：Beauty is more than skin deep. You need to look inside yourself.
　　　美貌不過一層皮，你需要更注重你的內在。

5. get one's beauty sleep　睡美容覺

哈哈：Can you be quiet? I'm gonna get my beauty sleep.
　　　妳可以安靜點嗎？我要睡我的美容覺了。

Lyla：Seriously? At two in the afternoon?
　　　你認真？下午兩點睡覺？

第 18 章　哈啦穿搭

角色：哈哈（來自台灣）、Lyla（來自美國）

你擅長穿搭嗎？你追求時尚嗎？現在，不管是平價時尚還是奢華時尚，各種潮流趨勢瞬息萬變，有些蔚為風潮，有些則是令人費解；有些人不惜花大錢緊跟潮流，有些人主張做自己就是潮！即使你認為以上這些都是無謂的浪費，一起來哈啦時尚也無傷大雅，至少讓自己在時尚界不至於成為文盲和啞巴！

1. Do you have any hoodies in stock?　你們有連帽衛衣嗎？

hoodie 連帽大學 T ／ in stock 有存貨

在這網購的時代，很多人買衣服還是偏好實體店面，畢竟實體購買時，試穿、物色還是比較方便的。首先，我們便來看看在服飾店購物的幾個公關金句吧！

• 關於「買衣服」，你還能這樣說：

I'm looking for some jeans.
我在找牛仔褲。

Does it come in blue?
它有藍色的嗎？

Can I try on a bigger one?
我可以試大一點的嗎？

look for 尋找	jeans 牛仔褲	come in 有
try on 試穿		

2. It's a little bit tight around the waist.　腰部有點緊。

tight 緊的／ waist 腰部

試穿時，如何表達「鬆」和「緊」呢？我們可以說：It's a little bit tight ／ loose around ＋部位．「在……部位有點緊／鬆。」而如果需要調整衣服，我們又該如何跟裁縫師傅說呢？記得「改短」是 take in、shorten 或 hem，如：Can you take in two centimeters for me?「你可以幫我改短兩公分嗎？」而「放長」則是 let out、let down 或 lengthen，如：I will let two centimeters down for you.「我

幫你放長兩公分。」最後，如果單純說「修改」衣服，我們可以用 alter 或 tailor 兩個動詞，如：I'd like to alter the dress shirt.「我想改這件西裝襯衫。」

• 關於「合身」，你還能這樣說：

The collar is kinda loose.
領口太鬆了。

The sleeves are not long enough.
袖子不夠長。

Looks like a good fit to me.
在我看來挺合身的！

collar 領口	loose 鬆的	sleeves 袖子
fit 合身		

3. They don't go together.　它們很不搭。

> go together 搭配好看

「搭配」我們可以用以下幾個動詞來表示：match、go together 和 go with。如：They go together well. 表示「它們很搭。」，而 They don't go together. 意思則是「它們不搭。」「混搭」則是 mix and match，如：You're really good at mixing and matching.「你好會混搭衣服。」

• 關於「搭配」，你還能這樣說：

I like it if you wear it with jeans.
這件搭牛仔褲的話我比較喜歡。

This color matches your jacket.
這個顏色和你的夾克很搭。

I think it goes well with your shirt.
我覺得它和你的襯衫很搭。

jeans 牛仔褲	match 搭配	jacket 夾克
shirt 襯衫	go well with 與……搭配	

4. That looks good on you.　你穿起來挺好看的！

> look　看起來

攜伴逛街的好處之一就是可以讓對方給自己一點建議，而當自己需要給對方建議時，你能說得出一朵花嗎？現在我們就來看看我們可以用哪些句子來讚美穿搭。最常聽到的，也是最簡單的可能是：You look good in that!「你穿起來挺好看的！」這句也可以說成：That looks good on you. 這邊介系詞使用的原則是「人＋ in ＋衣服」、「衣服＋ on ＋人」。另外，也可以說 It is a good look for you.「你穿起來很好看。」

* 關於「讚美穿搭」，你還能這樣說：

Nice dress!
妳的洋裝很好看！

It makes you look younger.
它讓你看起來更年輕。

You look smart!
你穿起來很漂亮！

dress　洋裝	smart　時髦、漂亮的

5. Why are you dressed like a giant bumblebee?
你幹嘛穿得像隻大黃蜂啊？

> dress　穿衣／ giant　巨大的／ bumblebee　大黃蜂

好友之間吐槽穿搭常常成為日常生活中的笑料。但吐槽要刻薄又要好笑該怎麼做到呢？來學學以下幾個句型吧！

* 關於「吐槽穿搭」，你還能這樣說：

When will you ever stop wearing black?
你什麼時候才能不穿黑色？

Don't you think you've overdressed yourself?
你不覺得你穿得太正式了嗎？

Don't tell me you're going like that! Go get changed!
別跟我說你要穿這樣出門！快去換掉！

| wear 穿著 | overdress 穿得過於正式 | change 換衣服 |

6. I always make sure I look nice and presentable before I leave the house. 我出門前一定會確定我的衣著是整潔美觀的。

> presentable 美觀的

很多人說：時尚是一種語言。的確，如果你時尚相關的詞彙量不足的話，即使英文說得再流利，講到這個話題時還是會像鴨子聽雷般，彷彿聽了另一種外語。以下，我們就來看看有哪些時尚造型相關的詞彙和句子是我們必須知道的。

[註]：常見造型風格的英文：preppy 學院風／ hipster 新潮的／ casual 休閒的／ business casual 商務休閒風／ sporty 運動風／ vintage 復古風／ minimalist 極簡風／ street style 街頭風／ exotic 異國風／ artsy 文藝風

• 關於「穿衣風格」，你還能這樣說：

He is a flip-flops, and event tee type of guy.
他是那種愛穿夾腳拖和活動 T 的宅男。

Because I work in an office, I usually dress in a business casual manner.
因為我是坐辦公室的，所以我的衣著都走商務休閒風。

I normally wear what suits me and things that reflect how I feel on the day.
我一般會穿適合我的還有能夠反映我當天心情的衣服。

flip-flops 夾腳拖	event tee 活動 T 恤	business casual 商務休閒
manner 方式	normally 一般	suit 適合
reflect 反映		

7. Suits You is my preferred source of nicer suits.

我買好一點的西裝一般都去 Suits You。

> preferred 較喜歡的／source 來源／suit 西裝

brand preference「品牌愛好」或「品牌傾向性」有時是有意識的，有時也有可能是不自覺的，就像走進巷口的早餐店那般自然，當然也有可能是懶得挑品牌啦！如果要説「我的……都……買的。」，我們可以説 I usually visit...for...，如：I usually visit Timberland for boots.「我的靴子通常都在 Timberland 買的。」

• 關於「品牌愛好」，你還能這樣説：

For shoes under 100 dollars, I usually shop at Shoes Valley.
一百元以下的鞋子，我一般都在 Shoes Valley 買。

Many of my ties are from Tie Rack.
我很多領帶都是在 Tie Rack 買的。

I'm a big fan of Adidas for trainers.
我很愛買愛迪達的運動鞋。

shop 購物	tie 領帶	fan 愛好者
trainers 運動鞋		

8. This scarf is a must-have item. 這條圍巾是一件必備單品。

> scarf 圍巾／must-have 必備的／item 品項

時尚潮流更新換代，每季都會有特定的必備單品。而關於「必備單品」的英文我們該怎麼表示呢？我們可以用上一個複合詞 must-have「必備的」。must-have 可作為形容詞或名詞，如：a must-have item「必備單品」、must-haves for fall「秋季必備單品」。另外，「秋季必備單品」我們還可以説 autumn essentials 或 autumn must-haves for your wardrobe「秋季必備服飾」。

• 關於「時尚必備」，你還能這樣説：

Browline sunglasses flatter everyone.
眉框太陽眼鏡每個人戴起來都好看。

A classic leather belt is one accessory that everyone should own.

一條經典的皮帶是每個人必備的一項配件。

I can't get enough of knee high boots.

高筒靴我怎麼穿都穿不膩。

browline sunglasses 眉框太陽眼鏡	flatter 使……好看	classic 經典的
leather belt 皮帶	accessory 配件	own 擁有
knee high boots 高筒靴	can't get enough of... 對……再多都不膩	

9. I have quite eclectic tastes in fashion. 我的時尚品味很多元。

eclectic 多元的／ taste 品味／ fashion 時尚

eclectic 這個詞的意思是「不拘一格的」、「兼容並蓄的」，拿來形容時尚品味
就是「多元的」的意思了，如：eclectic tastes in fashion「多元的時尚品味」，
也可以說 My taste is very eclectic.「我的品味很多元。」而「時尚品味」我們可
以用 fashion taste、fashion sense 或 sense of fashion 等，而「穿衣品味」我
們則可以說 dressing sense。

• 關於「時尚品味」，你還能這樣說：

He has a good dressing sense.

他的穿衣品味很好。

She's known for her bizarre sense of fashion.

她以她怪異的時尚品味聞名。

Fashion is a subjective matter.

時尚是很主觀的。

dressing 穿衣	sense 品味	bizarre 怪異的
subjective 主觀的	matter 事情	

10. Mikey is my fashion guru. Mikey 是我的時尚導師。

> guru 心靈導師

很多人相信 Fashion is a scam.「時尚是場騙局。」一切的時尚理念說到底都是要把手伸進消費者荷包裡的商人所編造出來的。儘管很多人心知肚明,但實際上還是心甘情願地追隨著各種雜誌、網紅,手指也停不了似的在各種購物軟體上瘋狂下單。在這種「一個願打,一個願挨」的現象中,存在著兩種角色:一是「潮流引領者」,英文叫 trend setter;一是「潮流追隨者」,英文是 trend follower。而「瘋狂追求時尚的人」,叫 fashionista,「盲目追求時尚的人」則是叫 fashion victim。

- 關於「追求時尚」,你還能這樣說:

Justin Timberlake is my greatest fashion influence.
Justin Timberlake 是在時尚方面影響我最深的名人。

He just copies celebrities' outfits.
他就只會模仿名人的穿著。

I like Jeff. He's my style role model.
我滿喜歡 Jeff 的,他是我的造型典範。

influence 影響	copy 模仿	celebrity 名人
outfit 服裝	style 造型	role model 典範

 跟時尚有關的慣用語

1. make a fashion statement 穿著新潮大膽

哈哈:Did you see what she wore? A rainbow T-shirt and hot-pants?
　　　妳看到她穿什麼了嗎?彩虹 T 配熱褲?

Lyla:She was trying to make a fashion statement.
　　　她想展現她的新潮時尚吧!

2. go out of style　退流行

哈哈：Why do you have so many pairs of identical jeans?
　　　妳為什麼有那麼多條一模一樣的牛仔褲？

Lyla：Well, you know…skinny jeans never go out of style.
　　　嗯⋯⋯你知道的！緊身牛仔褲永遠不會退流行啊！

3. fashion forward　衣著前衛的

哈哈：What is with your shoes? Trying to show you're a fashion forward woman.
　　　妳的鞋子怎麼了？想展示自己很前衛嗎？

Lyla：That's just dry paint that doesn't come off.
　　　那個只是洗不掉的油漆而已。

4. mutton dressed as lamb　打扮裝年輕

哈哈：Ms. Woodfield was wearing a mini-skirt today.
　　　Woodfield 女士今天穿了一件迷你裙。

Lyla：Can't imagine! She must have looked like mutton dressed as lamb.
　　　真無法想像！她是想裝年輕吧！

5. first in, best dressed　先得先贏

哈哈：I'm still wavering between Tennis Club and Dance Club.
　　　我還在考慮要加入網球社還是舞蹈社。

Lyla：You'd better decide now! It's always first in, best dressed.
　　　你最好現在就決定，每次都是先加入的能得到最多好處。

第 19 章　哈啦假期

角色：哈哈（來自台灣）、Lyla（來自美國）

假期總是那麼令人嚮往，又如此稍縱即逝。聊起假期計劃總能使人心情雀躍，假期泡湯則是讓人捶胸頓足，假期結束時又是那麼令人意志消沈。本章節我們就來學學各種聊假期的英文句子。

1. I'm mentally checked out already.　我的腦袋已經提前下班了。

mentally 心理上／ check out 打卡下班

嗡嗡嗡忙了一週後，終於熬到了星期五下午，這時很多人的腦袋應該都已經自動打卡下班了吧！這種心理提前打下班卡的心情，我們可以說：I'm mentally checked out already.「我的腦袋已經提前下班了。」或是 I'm already in the holiday mood.「我的心已經開始放假了。」下次放假前，不妨帶著雀躍的心情用上這個句子吧！

• 關於「假期前夕」，你還能這樣說：

TGI Friday. (Thank God It's Friday)
謝天謝地，終於星期五了！

This week has been crazy busy.
這週真的忙到瘋掉。

It's finally over!
終於結束了！

finally 終於	over 結束的

2. What are you doing for the long weekend?

你這個週末長假要做什麼？

> long weekend 連休三、四天的週末

放假前，和朋友、同事聊聊假期的安排，我們可以用上：What are you doing for the long weekend?「你這個週末長假要做什麼？」或是 What are you up to this weekend?「你這個週末有什麼計畫？」值得一提的是：在第一句中，因為是詢問即將發生的未來計畫，因此，我們可以用現在進行式代替未來式。而 long weekend 則是指連放三、四天的週末長假。

- 關於「詢問假期計畫」，你還能這樣說：

What's your plan for the holiday?
你這個假期有什麼計畫？

You got any plan for the weekend?
你這週末有安排嗎？

Are you going away this weekend?
你這週末要去哪裡嗎？

| plan 計畫 | have got 有 | go away 出行 |

3. I'm going downtown with Yusuf.　我要和 Yusuf 去市區。

> downtown 市區

如同第二句中提到的，關於即將發生的未來事件，我們可以用現在進行式代替未來式。因此，在敘述週末計畫時，我們也很常使用現在進行式的句型。如：
I'm going...、I'm staying here...、I'm painting my house... 等。以下，我們來看看更多談論假期計畫的句式。

- 關於「假期計畫」，你還能這樣說：

I'm thinking about going to Bangkok.
我在想要去曼谷。

I might hit the beach in Los Angeles.
我可能會去洛杉磯的海邊。

I'm planning on visiting my aunt in Edinburgh.
我計畫去愛丁堡找我阿姨。

hit 去	plan on 計畫

4. I might just stay home and relax. 我可能就宅在家休息。

relax 放鬆

如果你假期沒有什麼特別的安排，就只想宅在家休息，你可以說：I might ／ will just stay home and relax.「我可能就宅在家休息。」

• 關於「假期宅在家」，你還能這樣說：

I will just stay around here for the day.
我今天就待在這。

I'm not going anywhere.
我沒有要去哪。

I'll stay at home. I don't feel like going out.
我會待在家，不太想出門。

feel like 想要

5. I can't do much this weekend with the project I'm working on.
因為我手上的這個計畫，我這週末不太有空。

> project 計畫／ work on 從事

假期最悲催的事莫過於加班了。不管是主管臨時指派的工作還是當週的工作量爆表，不得不犧牲假期趕工，都讓人心情瞬間變得不美麗。這時當你的同事還在殘酷地問你假期計畫時，你便能向他投以一個厭世的眼神說：I can't do much with the project I'm working on.「因為我手上的這個計劃，我不太有空。」

• 關於「假期要工作」，你還能這樣說：

I'm working overtime this weekend.
我這週末要加班。

I don't think I'll have much free time this summer.
我這個夏天恐怕沒有多少空的時間。

I'm not as fortunate as you. I'll have to work the whole time.
我不像你那麼幸運，我一直都得工作。

overtime 加班	fortunate 幸運的	the whole time 一直

6. I was going to Kenting but my plan fell through at the last minute because of the typhoon.
我原本要去墾丁的，但最後因為颱風，計畫泡湯了。

> fall through 失敗／ at the last minute 最後關頭

俗話說的好：計劃永遠趕不上變化。很多時候，一個月前就規劃好的假期往往會因為各種原因無法實現，而 last minute「最後一分鐘」的臨時起意反而比較能夠成行。當你事前規劃好的假期計劃因為突發事件而有所變動時，你便能用上這個句子。其中，I was going to... 用了過去進行式表示「原本要去……」。

• 關於「假期計畫變動」，你還能這樣說：

We were originally leaving on Saturday but because of the shift change we brought it forward to Friday.
我們原本是星期六出發的，但我的班有變動，所以我們改到星期五出發。

My boss gave me extra work, so I'll have to put off my holiday.

我老闆又給我加工作，所以我要把我的假期延期了。

Look at this rain! Seems like I have to call off my trip.

這雨勢……看來我必須取消我的旅行了。

originally 原本	shift 輪班	bring forward ……將……提前
extra 額外的	put off 推遲	seems like 似乎
call off 取消		

7. I'm having a hard time combating the Monday blues.

我正與星期一症候群搏鬥中。

> have a hard time 做……很困難／ combat 對抗／
> the Monday blues 星期一症候群

很多上班族都有感：假期總是過得和光速一樣快，而週一總是走得比龜速還慢。「星期一症候群」是所有辛苦的上班族共同的天敵。從星期天晚上萌發的消沉感、星期一早上千斤重的眼皮子，到前往公司的漫漫長路，都使得人們對週一早晨充滿恐懼。這種與憂鬱星期一抗戰的心情，你可以這麼說：I'm having a hard time combating the Monday blues.「我正與星期一症候群搏鬥中。」

• 關於「假期結束症候群」，你還能這樣說：

I'm having all the symptoms of the Monday morning blues.

我現在全身上下都是星期一症候群的症狀。

I always feel sluggish on Monday morning.

我星期一早上老是很懶散。

I almost slept in.

我差點睡過頭。

symptom 症狀	sluggish 懶散的	sleep in 睡過頭

8. Where did you go for your last holiday?　你上個假期去哪兒玩了？

last 上一個

假期結束後，和朋友、同事們分享一下自己的假期過得如何，也許是個緩解週一憂鬱症候群的方法。問朋友：「假期上哪兒去玩了？」你可以這樣問：

Where did you go for your last holiday?

* 關於「上個假期」，你還能這樣說：

Who did you go there with?
你和誰去的？

Did you have a good time there?
那邊好玩嗎？

Did you enjoy your holiday?
你假期過得開心嗎？

have a good time 玩得開心

9. What was your favorite holiday in your life?
你到目前為止最喜歡的是哪一段假期？

favorite 最喜歡的

美食和旅行往往是聊天時失敗率極低的話題。和別人聊到過去的假期時，可以學學這幾個問句。記得都要用過去式喔！

* 關於「以前的假期」，你還能這樣說：

What was your worst holiday experience?
你最糟糕的假期是哪一段？

How long ago was that?
那是多久之前的事？

What was the most memorable thing that happened during the holiday?

在那段假期中，令你印象最深刻的事是什麼？

worst 最糟的	experience 經驗	memorable 難忘的

10. Do you have a holiday due at any point?

你這陣子有什麼假期計畫嗎？

> due 預期的

想要消除假期逝去的空虛感嗎？那就來聊聊下一次的假期規劃啊！詢問對方最近的假期計劃，我們可以說：Do you have a holiday due at any point? 其中，due 是指「預期要發生的」的意思。

- 關於「下一次假期」，你還能這樣說：

When's your next holiday?

你的下一次假期是什麼時候？

Where are you going next?

你下次要去哪裡？

What's your plan for the next holiday?

你下一次的假期計畫是什麼？

plan 計畫

1. get itchy feet　蠢蠢欲動

哈哈：Finally it's Friday!

終於星期五了！

Lyla：Yeah! I've started to get itchy feet!

對啊！我的心已經開始蠢蠢欲動想出遊了！

2. chillax　放鬆

哈哈：I've been working nonstop for two weeks. I'm exhausted.

我已經連續工作兩星期了，我好累。

Lyla：You really need to chillax a bit.

你真的需要休息一下。

3. put one's feet up　放鬆

哈哈：After the past two hectic months, I need to sit back and put my feet up for the whole holiday.

經過了兩個月的折騰，我這整個假期需要徹底地放鬆一下。

Lyla：But you promised to help me move.

你不是答應要幫我搬家嗎？

4. footloose and fancy-free　心無罣礙

哈哈：It feels so good to be footloose and fancy-free.

這樣心無罣礙的感覺真棒。

Lyla：Your boss just called and asked about the project.

你老闆剛剛打電話來問你方案做得怎麼樣。

5. have a blast　玩得很開心

哈哈：Lyla, what did you do over the weekend?

Lyla，妳週末做了什麼？

Lyla：I went to Susana's drinking and watching movies. We had a blast.

我去了 Susana 家喝酒、看電影，玩得超開心。

第 20 章　哈啦旅行

角色：哈哈（來自台灣）、Lyla（來自美國）

俗話説：在家靠父母，出門靠張嘴。雖然現在旅遊出行時，大家其實都是靠手機、靠網路，但既然都出門旅遊了，何不放下螢幕，開啟離線模式，用雙眼感受一下真實的世界，用語言和活生生的人交流呢？有時候，旅行中一次偶然的問路，還可能邂逅出一段美好的友誼或愛情呢！這也許才是旅遊最大的收穫吧！本章節，我們就一起來學學超好用的旅遊英文會話吧！

1. Getting excited about your trip?　要去玩了開心嗎？

> excited　感到興奮的／ trip　旅行

朋友出行前，我們上前關心一下行李收拾得怎麼樣、什麼時候出發、行前心情如何等，以下幾個句子都是相當自然而地道的對話啟動器喔。

• 關於「詢問旅遊計劃」，你還能這樣說：

Are you all packed yet?
你都打包好了嗎？

When are you heading off?
你什麼時候出發？

Are you going on a tour or on your own?
你要跟團還是自助旅行？

pack 打包	head off 出發	tour 遊覽

2. The Eiffel Tower is a must-see.　艾菲爾鐵塔是一個必去行程。

> Eiffel Tower　艾菲爾鐵塔／ must-see　必看行程

跟朋友推薦旅行景點的時候，有沒有彷彿那個景點是自己家開的一樣呢？沒錯！雖然不是自己要去玩，但推薦自己曾經去過的地方時，真的有種彷彿是自己要出遊的錯覺，心裡的興奮程度真的不輸真正要去玩的人呢！以下幾個句子，讓你能夠完美地表達推薦旅遊景點時心中溢滿出來的「莫名的」興奮感。

- 關於「推薦旅遊景點」，你還能這樣說：

Check out the night markets. They're amazing.
一定要去逛夜市，夜市超棒的。

You can't miss the amazing street foods in Taipei.
你一定不能錯過台北的美味小吃。

You must go to Clifton Suspension Bridge.
你一定要去 Clifton 吊橋。

night market 夜市	miss 錯過	street food 街頭小吃
check out 查看	suspension bridge 吊橋	

3. I've always wanted to go to Los Angeles.　我一直很想去洛杉磯。

Los Angeles 洛杉磯

很多人心中一定都有自己最嚮往的旅行，不管是想去的地方、想走的路線或鍾意的行程。和朋友聊旅行時，用以下幾句來表達自己的旅行取向，偵測一下朋友圈中有沒有適合自己的旅友吧！本句 I've always wanted to go to... 表示「我一直都想去……。」用在表達想去一個自己還沒去過的地方。

- 關於「旅行取向」，你還能這樣說：

I prefer those all-inclusive kinds of vacations.
我更喜歡那種全包制的旅遊行程。

I'm not really a country person.
我不太喜歡走鄉村的行程。

I'd rather have a relaxing staycation.
我寧願在家宅度假。

prefer 更喜歡	all-inclusive 全包制的	country 鄉村
would rather 寧願	relaxing 令人放鬆的	staycation 宅度假

4. Safe travels.　一路平安。

> safe　安全的

出行前，給家人、朋友、甚至是問路的陌生人送上一句簡單誠摯的祝福吧！祝他們一路平安、順飛、旅行愉快。以下幾句都非常常用，任君挑選！本句 Safe travels. 也可說 Travel safe. 表示「一路平安。」其他像是法語的 Bon voyage. 和可愛的小孩用語 See you later, alligator. 也很常聽到喔！

• 關於「祝福旅行平安」，你還能這樣說：

Have a safe flight. Let me know when you land.
順飛，降落時告訴我。

Enjoy the journey.
玩得開心。

Wishing you a safe journey.
祝你旅途平安。

flight 飛行	land 降落	journey 旅行
wish 祝願		

5. Excuse me. We're looking for Taipei Main Station.
不好意思，我們在找臺北車站。

> look for　尋找

旅行中，最常需要與人交談的時機應該就是問路了。（除了問手機地圖之外。）以下幾句都是你不能不知道的問路英語。記得，問路前別忘了加一句 Excuse me.「不好意思。」才不會嚇到別人囉！

• 關於「旅行中問路」，你還能這樣說：

Can you tell me where Central Park is?
請問中央公園怎麼去？

Can you tell me how to get to the closest metro station?
請問最近的地鐵站怎麼去？

Excuse me. I'm lost. Can you help me?

不好意思，我迷路了，可以請你幫忙一下嗎？

lost 迷路的	metro station 地鐵站

6. Excuse me. Is this the train for New Swanstone Castle?

不好意思，請問這班車是到新天鵝堡的嗎？

New Swanstone Castle 新天鵝堡

在人生地不熟的國外搭各種交通工具很常會出現趕時間、標誌看不懂或找不到路的慌亂情景。這時候，我們一定要盡力保持冷靜，熟記以下這幾句旅行中搭車的救命金句，避免搭錯車、下錯站的窘境。

• 關於「旅行中搭車」，你還能這樣說：

Excuse me. Is this the train bound for Palo Alto?

不好意思，請問這班火車是到帕羅奧圖的嗎？

Excuse me. Does this bus go to Beverly Hills?

不好意思，請問這班車會到比佛利山莊嗎？

Excuse me. I need to get to Chinatown. When do I get off?

不好意思，我要去中國城，請問我該什麼時候下車？

bound 往	Palo Alto 帕羅奧圖	Beverly Hills 比佛利山莊
Chinatown 中國城	get off 下車	

7. Excuse me. I'm looking for the restroom.

不好意思，請問洗手間在哪裡？

> look for 尋找／ restroom 洗手間

除了問路、搭車等相對重要的情境，旅行中還會遇到許多只要開口就能輕鬆解決問題的時刻，諸如：問洗手間在哪、拍照、推薦景點等。學英文的過程中，往往就是這種成功讓對方聽懂自己的時刻最能帶來成就感了。

• 關於「旅遊中的大小事」，你還能這樣說：

Can you take a picture for me please?
可以幫我拍張照嗎？

Excuse me. Do you speak English?
不好意思，請問你說英文嗎？

What places would you recommend to visit in Melbourne?
你有推薦什麼墨爾本的景點嗎？

recommend 推薦	Melbourne 墨爾本

8. Beijing is a fascinating city with many historical landmarks.

北京是一座擁有很多古蹟的迷人城市。

> Beijing 北京／ fascinating 迷人的／ historical 歷史的／ landmark 地標

旅行歸來後的第一個上班上學日，有誰不會和朋友同事大聊自己的旅行斬獲呢？以下幾個實用金句，讓你自行替換地點！其中，形容城市，我們可以用上以下幾個形容詞：fascinating「迷人的」、charming「迷人的」、exciting「有趣的」、interesting「有趣的」、wonderful「美好的」。

• 關於「愉快的旅行經驗」，你還能這樣說：

Fisherman's Wharf was one of my favorites.
漁人碼頭是我最愛的景點之一。

Taiwan's got great food.
台灣的美食超讚的。

It was like nowhere I'd ever been before.
它和我去過的其他地方都不一樣。

| wharf 碼頭 | favorite 最喜歡的事物 | nowhere 任何地方都不 |

9. It wasn't my cup of tea, but it was still a nice place.
我個人是覺得還好，但它還是一個不錯的地方。

> one's cup of tea 某人鍾意的人事物

如果去到一些普普通通、不太好玩的地方，我們可以說：...is not my cup of tea.「我覺得……還好。」其中，one's cup of tea 這個片語表示「某人喜歡的人事物」。比如：She's not my cup of tea. 意思就是「她不是我喜歡的類型。」還可以說成：She's not my style. 或 She's not my type.

• 關於「不太好的旅行經驗」，你還能這樣說：

I wasn't so keen on the floating market.
我對水上市場不太有興趣。

It's too developed and touristy.
它有點過度開發並且太觀光化了。

I wish it'd been less crowded.
要是當時人沒有那麼多就更好了。

| be keen on 對……感興趣 | develop 開發 | touristy 適合觀光的 |
| wish 但願 | less 更不 | crowded 擁擠的 |

10. What trip do you have coming up?　你接下來有什麼旅遊計劃？

> come up　來臨

最後，回到日常生活中，和別人聊聊過去和將來的旅行時，我們有可能談到：接下來的旅行計劃、最想去哪些國家、去過最好玩的地方等。參考一下別人的旅行藍圖，為自己的下一次壯遊汲取些靈感吧！

- 關於「過去和未來的旅行」，你還能這樣說：

What countries would you most like to visit?
你最想去哪些國家？

What was your favorite ever place in your whole life?
你此生最愛的地方是哪裡？

Is there somewhere in the world that you're desperate to see that you haven't seen yet?
哪裡是你一直想去但還沒去到過的地方？

> desperate　極度渴望的

跟旅遊有關的慣用語

1. off the beaten track　鮮為人知、人跡罕至

哈哈：Do you think we'll be able to get the tickets to the museum?
　　　妳覺得我們買得到那間博物館的門票嗎？

Lyla：Absolutely! It's really off the beaten track.
　　　當然可以！那裡真的很少人會去。

2. hit the road 上路

Lyla：Hurry up! We should hit the road before the highway becomes a parking lot.
快點！我們要在高速公路塞車前趕快上路。

哈哈：No, that must hurt!
不要！那一定很痛！

3. travel on a shoestring 窮遊

哈哈：Did you spend a lot in India?
妳去印度花了很多錢嗎？

Lyla：Not at all. I was traveling on a shoestring.
沒有，我當時去窮遊的。

4. catch the sun 曬傷

哈哈：Look at my perfect tan!
看看我曬得多美！

Lyla：It looks like you caught the sun.
看起來根本像是曬傷。

5. There is no place like home. 金窩銀窩還不如自己的狗窩。

哈哈：Finally made it back!
終於回來了！

Lyla：There is no place like home, huh?
還是家裡好吧！？

第 21 章 哈啦旅館

角色：哈哈（來自台灣）、Lyla（來自美國）

即使是一個人的旅行，入住旅館必定是一個需要與人接觸、交流的環節。不管是隱私性較高的星級飯店還是多人共住的青年旅社，住宿的過程即是對語言及語用能力的高度考驗。想要從預訂、入住、諮詢、投訴到退房等各個環節溝通順暢無阻嗎？現在，我們就一起來學習旅館住宿相關的英文會話吧！

1. I have a reservation for a single room for two nights.
我預訂了一間兩晚的單人房。

> reservation 預定／ single room 單人房

首先，我們來說說訂房。很多人應該都學過「預訂」的英文可以用 reserve、book 和 make a reservation，但真正使用的時候還是會出現搭配語上的小錯誤。因此，還是建議大家將整個句子都練起來：I have a reservation for a ＋房型＋ for ＋天數 .；I have booked a ＋房型＋ for ＋日期＋ for ＋天數。通常櫃檯人員此時會回一句：Okay. Let me look that up for you. 「好的，我來幫您看看。」

[註]：各種房型的英文：single room 單人房 / double room 雙人房 / twin room 雙床房 / triple room 三人房 / family room 家庭房 / adjoining room 連通房 / suite 套房

• 關於「訂旅館」，你還能這樣說：

I'd like to book a room for May 5th for three nights please.
我想要訂一間五月五日三個晚上的房間。

I have a reservation for today. The name is Lin.
我今天有預訂，名字是林。

Hi. I have a reservation and I'm checking in.
您好，我有預訂，現在要入住。

book 預訂	available 可得到的

2. I made the booking on the Internet.　我是在網路上預訂的。

> booking 預定／ Internet 網路

入住或打電話確認預訂時，時常需要提供相關的預訂資訊，包含預訂方式、訂單編號或姓名等。關於預訂方式，我們可以說：I made the booking on ＋平台名稱。訂單編號的英文則是 reservation number；而預訂姓名通常會和介系詞 under 搭配，如：I have a reservation under the name of Lee.「我用李這個名字訂了間房。」現場辦理入住時，櫃檯人員通常會問：May I see some IDs, please?「我可以看一下您的證件嗎？」這時，我們便需要出示護照 passport 或駕照 driver's license。

- 關於「確認預定資訊」，你還能這樣說：

I booked it directly through you.
我是直接向你們預訂的。

I have a reservation number if that helps.
我有訂單編號如果您需要的話。

I've already paid the deposit for the first night.
我已經付了第一晚的訂金。

directly 直接地	through 透過	reservation number 訂單編號
already 已經	deposit 訂金	

3. I'd like to have a room with a view of the ocean.
我想要一間海景房。

> view 景觀

自助旅行時，有時住宿是到了當地才臨時找的，這時，我們可以問旅館櫃台：Do you have any rooms available for today?「請問你們今天有空房嗎？」如果有空房，櫃台人員可能會問你：What type of room would you like?「您想要什麼樣的房型？」我們便能回答：I'd like (to have) a ＋房型 .。

- 關於「現場訂房」，你還能這樣說：

Is there anything available for today?
你們今大有空房嗎？

What's the rate for the room?
房費是多少？

Is there any way you could offer a discount?
可以給我點折扣嗎？

available 可得到的	rate 房費	discount 折扣

4. Do you offer shuttle service?　你們有提供接駁車嗎？

offer 提供／ shuttle 接駁車／ service 服務

詢問旅館提供的服務，最常用的句型便是：Do you offer...?「你們有提供……嗎？」如：Do you offer a shuttle service?「你們有提供接駁車嗎？」、Do you offer valet parking service?「你們有提供代客泊車服務嗎？」、Do you offer free breakfast?「你們有提供免費早餐嗎？」為了表示禮貌，我們可以在每個問句之前加上：I wanted to ask...「我想問一下……」。其中，want 用了過去式可以表達出委婉的語氣。

- 關於「詢問旅館服務」，你還能這樣說：

Can I leave my luggage here?
我可以把行李寄放在這嗎？

I wanted to ask: what time is breakfast?
請問一下：早餐是幾點提供？

I'd like a wake-up call tomorrow morning if possible.
我想要明天早上的喚醒服務。

leave 存留	luggage 行李	wake-up call 喚醒服務
possible 可能的		

5. What kinds of gym facilities do you have?　你們有哪些健身設施？

> gym　健身房／ facility　設施

除了特定的服務外，旅館的公共設施也是許多人住宿時非常關切的點，特別是對於出差人員或有健身習慣的旅客。除了 Do you offer...? 之外，我們還可以用上 What kinds of... facilities do you have?「你們有哪些……設施？」

- 關於「詢問旅館設施」，你還能這樣說：

Do you offer conferencing facilities?
你們有提供會議設備嗎？

Do you have laundry services?
你們有洗衣服務嗎？

Is there a swimming pool in this hotel?
這間旅館有游泳池嗎？

conferencing 開會的	facility 設施	laundry 洗衣房

6. May I have the wifi password?　請問一下 wifi 密碼是什麼？

> password　密碼

wifi 密碼應該是所有的現代人入住旅館時最關心的「生命攸關」的話題了！因此，這句救命金句：May I have the wifi password?「請問一下 wifi 密碼是什麼？」可一定要學起來啊！

- 關於「詢問 wifi」，你還能這樣說：

Do you have free wifi?
你們有免費 wifi 嗎？

Excuse me. Which one do I connect to?
不好意思，請問是連接哪一個？

What about wireless Internet?

請問有無線網路嗎？

connect 連接	wireless 無線的

7. I need some restaurant recommendations.

我需要一些餐廳推薦的資訊。

restaurant 餐廳／ recommendation 推薦

一般典型的配置齊全的旅館都會有協助辦理入住和退房的櫃檯人員 receptionist 以及提供周邊旅遊、交通、餐飲諮詢和訂票服務的禮賓服務員 concierge。如果你是初來乍到一個陌生的城市，又沒有提前做旅遊攻略的話，就可以向 hotel concierge 諮詢一下附近好吃、好玩的景點，這時，你需要的句型便是：I need some...recommendations.「我需要一些……的資訊。」

• 關於「詢問各種資訊」，你還能這樣說：

Can you tell me some nice places to go to around here?

你可以告訴我這附近有什麼好玩的景點嗎？

Hello! I was told that I could get some sightseeing advice from you.

您好！我被告知我可以請教您一些這附近觀光的建議。

I wanted to ask: what is the quickest way to get to the airport?

我想請問一下：去機場最快的方式是什麼？

sightseeing 觀光	advice 建議	quick 快速的
airport 機場		

8. There is an issue with the shower.　淋浴間有一點問題。

issue　問題／shower　淋浴間

當發現旅館有問題，需要回報前台處理時，我們可以說：I'd like to make a complaint.「我要客訴。」我們通常會用到 problem 或 issue 這兩個字，兩者都有「問題」的意思。相關的句型為：There is an issue with... 或 There is a problem with...「……有一點問題。」

• 關於「回報問題」，你還能這樣說：

I have a few problems with my room.
我的房間有一些問題。

Something's wrong with my curtain.
我的窗簾有一點問題。

I'm not sure if it's normal, but I think there's a problem with the phone.
我不確定這樣是不是正常的，但我覺得電話有點問題。

curtain　窗簾	normal　正常的

9. Hi. I'd like to check out.　您好，我要退房。

check out　退房

退房的英語很簡單，我們可以直接說：I'd like to check out. 或 I'm checking out.「我要退房。」如果櫃檯人員問：Did you enjoy your stay? 或 How did you enjoy your stay?「請問您住得滿意嗎？」通常我們可以回答：Yes, I enjoyed it. 或 It was fantastic. 來表達「非常滿意」。

• 關於「退房」，你還能這樣說：

What time is check out?
請問幾點退房？

What time must I check out?

請問我幾點得退房？

Is it possible if I check out one hour late?

請問我可以晚一個小時退房嗎？

possible 可能的

10. **Here you go.** 請拿去。

here you go 請拿去

在和旅館服務員對話時，只會說 OK 和 Yes 嗎？學學這幾句，讓自己的語言表現更加豐富吧！不僅在旅館，許多其他語境都適用的喔！本句 Here you go. 可用在櫃檯人員向我們要證件或其他任何遞東西給別人時的回覆。

• 關於「回應旅館人員」，你還能這樣說：

Wonderful! Thanks for your help.

太好了，感謝你的幫忙。

Perfect. Thank you.

太好了，謝謝你。

That could work.

那樣可以。

wonderful 極好的	perfect 完美的

1. low season　淡季

哈哈：Check this out. The luxury suite is only 100 dollars.

看看這個，豪華套房只要一百元欸！

Lyla：It's low season. Everything is cheaper right now.

現在是淡季，什麼東西都很便宜。

2. B &B (Bed-and-Breakfast)　民宿（住宿加早餐旅店）

哈哈：Did you stay in hotels during your holiday in Thailand?

妳這次去泰國度假都是住飯店嗎？

Lyla：No. I stayed at a bed-and-breakfast cause I was traveling on a budget.

不是，我都住民宿，因為我預算有限。

3. infinity pool　無邊際泳池

哈哈：What was your favorite facility in the hotel?

這間旅館妳最喜歡的設施是什麼？

Lyla：Definitely the rooftop infinity pool. The view was so great!

當然是頂樓無邊際泳池囉！景觀超讚的！

4. ocean-front　海景房

Receptionist：What type of room would you like?

您想要什麼樣的房型呢？

Lyla：I'd like an ocean-front if possible.

我想要海景房。

5. all-inclusive　全包式住宿

哈哈：I prefer to spend my whole holiday staying in one place and just relaxing.

我喜歡整個假期就在一個地方待著好好放鬆。

Lyla：I think an all-inclusive resort will suit you.

那我覺得全包式度假村很適合你。

第 22 章　哈啦搭飛機

角色：哈哈（來自台灣）、Lyla（來自美國）

搭飛機對某些人來說可能是旅行中最令人期待的行程，但對於患有「恐飛症」的人來說卻可能是最大的惡夢。而機場作為長途旅行中必經的站點，可能是新奇，同時也可能是令人焦躁的。尤其是在人生地不熟的外國機場，如果又加上語言不通，那確實是場令人手足無措的闖關遊戲啊！今天就讓我們一起來聊聊關於搭飛機的各種英語會話，讓我們在旅行前儲備好自己的語言能力吧！

1. I'm flying Delta Airlines. 我搭達美航空。

fly 搭飛機／ airline 航空公司

首先，在到達機場時，我們通常可以看到機場的工作人員或航空公司的地勤人員。此時，我們便可以向他們詢問各種航班的資訊，如：航廈、值機櫃檯的位置或辦理值機的各種流程。如本句：I'm flying Delta Airlines. 或 I'm flying with Delta Airlines.「我搭達美航空。」地勤人員聽到，便會將我們指引到指定航空的值機櫃檯。

• 關於「到達機場」，你還能這樣說：

Excuse me. What terminal is for international flights?
不好意思，請問國際航班是在哪個航廈？

Excuse me. Where's the Singapore Airlines check-in counter?
不好意思，請問新加坡航空的櫃檯在哪？

I've checked in online. Do I need to print out my boarding pass?
我已經辦理線上值機了，我還需要把登機證印出來嗎？

terminal 航廈	international 國際的	flight 班機
check-in counter 值機櫃檯	online 線上	print 列印
boarding pass 登機證		

2. I have a flight that leaves in about three hours.

我的班機大約在三個小時後起飛。

> leave 離開

由於各種原因，我們可能會需要向別人說明或詢問自己的航班資訊，如：登機時間、起飛時間、轉機時長等。我們可以將這幾句背起來，再根據情況替換臨場資訊。如本句：I have a flight that leaves in about three hours.「我的班機大約在三個小時後起飛。」我們可以替換成：I have a flight that departs from Terminal One.「我的班機從第一航廈起飛。」或 I have a flight that departs from Gate 22.「我的班機從 22 號登機門起飛。」

- 關於「航班資訊」，你還能這樣說：

I will have a two-hour layover in Busan.
我會在釜山轉機兩個小時。

My final destination is Istanbul.
我要去伊斯坦堡。

I missed my flight. When is the next available flight?
我錯過我的班機了。下一班我能搭的飛機是什麼時候？

layover 轉機	Busan 釜山	destination 目的地
Istanbul 伊斯坦堡	miss 錯過	available 可得到的

3. How many suitcases can I check in?　我可以托運幾個行李箱？

> suitcase 行李箱／ check in 辦理托運

順利找到值機櫃檯後，便可以排隊等待辦理值機或行李托運。關於「行李」，我們可以說 luggage 或 baggage，這兩個詞皆不可數，必須用單位來表示複數，如：two pieces of luggage.「兩件行李」或直接用可數的 suitcase 或 bag 來表示。搭飛機時，行李分為：checked bags「托運行李」和 carry-on bags「登機行李」。關於兩種行李的件數和尺寸的規定，各家航空公司不盡相同，行前務必得查閱並確認清楚。

行李秤重時，地勤人員會說：Please place your luggage on the scale.「請將您的行李放在秤上。」當托運行李超重時，旅客必須支付 EBC（Excess Baggage Charge），即「超額行李費」。

• 關於「行李」，你還能這樣說：

How many bags can I bring on?
我可以帶幾個包上飛機？

How much is the excess?
超重費多少？

Let me take a few things out.
我把一些東西拿出來。

excess　超過的部分

4. I got bumped up to first class.　　我被升級到頭等艙了。

get bumped up　被升等／ first class　頭等艙

登機一般有三種方式：線上登機、自助櫃檯登機及人工櫃檯登機。線上登機的開放時間也是根據各家航空公司的規定，如：起飛前三十個小時起。如果想變更線上登機時的選位，可再到人工櫃檯變更座位。有時，因為機位超賣等原因，某些旅客能幸運地被升等機位，這時候我們便能說：I got bumped up to first class ／ business class.「我被升級到頭等艙／商務艙了。」

[註]：各種艙等的英文：economy class 經濟艙／ business class 商務／ first class 頭等艙

• 關於「機位」，你還能這樣說：

Can I get an aisle seat?
可以給我靠走道的座位嗎？

I'd like to sit together with my friend if that's possible.
我想和我的朋友坐在一起。

Can I change my seat?
我可以換座位嗎？

aisle　走道	seat　座位

5. What is the gate number again?　您剛剛說是幾號登機門？

> gate　登機門

登機結束前，地勤人員通常會在登機證上標示出登機時間、起飛時間及登機門號碼。如果因為對方說太快而沒有聽清楚，我們可以用本句來確認：What is the gate number again? 或 What did you say the gate number is?「您剛剛說是幾號登機門？」

- 關於「登機門」，你還能這樣說：

Where is gate A5?
請問 A5 登機門在哪裡？

How do I get to gate C1?
請問 C1 登機門怎麼走？

When should I be at the gate?
請問我什麼時候要抵達登機門？

> get to　抵達

6. I'd like to exchange 50,000 Taiwanese dollars to US dollars.
我想把五萬台幣換成美金。

> exchange　兌換

取得登機證後，我們便可開始換錢、購物、吃東西。其中，機場的貨幣兌換處叫做：money exchange 或 currency exchange。換匯時，我們可以記下這個句型：I'd like to exchange...to...「我想把……幣換成……幣。」

- 關於「機場設施及服務」，你還能這樣說：

Where can I find a duty free shop?
請問免稅店在哪？

Is there somewhere to eat around here?
請問這附近有賣吃的嗎？

I'd like to ask you about this cake. Is it popular as a souvenir?

我想請問一下：這個蛋糕適合當作紀念品嗎？

taxi 計程車	somewhere 某處	popular 受歡迎的
souvenir 紀念品		

7. Do I need to take my laptop out of the bag?

我需要把筆電拿出來嗎？

> laptop 筆記型電腦

登機前，我們還必須通過一個重要的關卡：安檢。一般而言，經驗豐富的旅客都知道安檢時的相關要求及流程，因此，在這個關卡基本上不太需要與人交談。但如果你是位搭飛機的新手或不幸遇上趕飛機的情況，在現場可能就需要這幾個救命金句了。

除此之外，你也需要能聽得懂以下幾句：Come on through.「請過來。」、Place your laptop in a separate tray.「把筆電放在另一個籃子裡。」、Stand on the mark on the floor and raise your arms.「站在標記上，舉起雙臂。」、Do you have anything in your pocket?「你的口袋有東西嗎？」、We need to search your bag.「我們需要檢查一下你的包。」、I'm afraid I have to take this bottle.「我必須拿走你的這個瓶子。」

• 關於「過安檢」，你還能這樣說：

Do I need to take off my shoes?
我需要脫鞋嗎？

I'm really late for my flight. Can I go to the front of the line?
我快趕不上我的飛機了，我可以插隊一下嗎？

I've got through security.
我通過安檢了。

take off 脫掉	line 隊伍	get through 通過
security 安檢		

8. How long is the flight delayed? 請問班機延誤多久？

> delay 使延誤

搭飛機難免會遇到班機延誤，如果不影響行程，那便能趁機逛逛免稅店、滑滑手機、看看電影；如果有可能影響接下來的行程，那就需要向地勤人員問清楚了。問「班機延誤多久」，我們可以說：How long is the flight delayed? 或 How long is the delay?

• 關於「班機延誤」，你還能這樣說：

How long do we have to wait?
請問我們要等多久？

Why is the flight delayed?
為什麼班機會延誤？

When do you expect the flight to depart?
請問這個班機什麼時候起飛？

expect 預期	depart 離開

9. Can I have a blanket? 可以給我一條毯子嗎？

> blanket 毯子

順利登機了！在飛機上，和空服員交流就可以放輕鬆一點了。和空服員點餐或要東西，我們可以用：Can I have a...?「可以給我一個……嗎？」如：Can I have a blanket?「可以給我一條毯子嗎？」、Can I have some water please?「可以給我水嗎？」、Can I have a pair of earbuds?「可以給我耳塞嗎？」另外，送餐時，當空服員問：Would you like chicken or beef?「請問您要雞肉還是牛肉的？」我們可以回答：I'll have the...「請給我……的。」

• 關於「機上服務」，你還能這樣說：

When will dinner be served?
請問什麼時候上晚餐？

Do you have a vegetarian option?
你們有提供素食餐嗎？

I'll have the beef.
我要牛肉的。

serve 上餐	vegetarian 素食的	option 選項

10. I have a business meeting in Portland. 我在波特蘭有一場商務會議。

business meeting 商務會議／Portland 波特蘭

飛機順利抵達後，我們還剩最後一關，那就是：入境過海關。有些 customs officer「海關人員」根本什麼都不會問就蓋章讓人通過了，有些則是會問得比較仔細，如：What is the purpose of your visit?「你來……的目的是什麼？」、How long are you staying?「你要待多久？」、Where will you be staying?「你會住在哪？」等。不過不用緊張，只要清楚、誠實地回答，一般都能順利過關的！

• 關於「入境過海關」，你還能這樣說：

I'm here on business.
我來出差的。

I'm visiting some friends.
我來拜訪朋友。

I'm just on holiday.
我來度假的。

on business 出差	visit 拜訪	on holiday 度假

跟搭飛機有關的慣用語：

1. take off　事業起飛

哈哈：Jam is joining the military. We won't get to see him for the
　　　next two years.
　　　Jam 要去當兵了，我們之後兩年都看不到他了。

Lyla：That's a shame. His career just began to take off.
　　　真可惜，他的事業才剛剛起飛呢！

2. redeye flight　紅眼航班

哈哈：You look so tired. What happened?
　　　妳看起來好累，怎麼了嗎？

Lyla：I caught a redeye flight from Los Angeles back here.
　　　我剛從洛杉磯搭了一班紅眼班機飛回來。

3. fly under the radar　行事低調，不引人注意

哈哈：Have you met the new assistant manager? What's she like?
　　　妳見過那位新來的副理嗎？她人怎麼樣？

Lyla：She likes to fly under the radar. Nobody knows her a lot.
　　　她一向行事低調，沒有人跟她熟。

4. fly into a rage　大發雷霆

哈哈：What would happen if you told your father you quit your job?
　　　如果妳告訴妳爸爸妳辭職了，他會怎麼樣？

Lyla：He will definitely fly into a rage.
　　　他一定會大發雷霆。

5. on the fly　不假思索地做某事

哈哈：I heard you ran into your boss while you were skiving off.
　　　我聽說妳翹班的時候撞見妳的老闆了。

Lyla：Yeah, so I quickly made up an excuse on the fly.
　　　對啊！所以我當下馬上編了一個藉口。

第23章　哈啦拍照

角色：哈哈（來自台灣）、Lyla（來自美國）

恐怕沒有一個時代比現在更流行拍照了，尤其當智慧型手機的拍照鏡頭一支比一支逆天強大，濾鏡一個比一個魔幻智能，當上零死角網紅已經再也不是夢。在這個拍照已成為顯學的今天，生活中處處充滿著需要用英文來哈啦拍照的時機，今天我們就果斷地來背幾句拍照相關的英文句子吧！

1. Pictures time.　來拍照囉！

> picture　照片

...time 可以用來招喚大家一起去做某件事情，比如：dinner time 表示「吃晚餐囉」、soccer time 表示「踢足球囉」，而呼喚大家來拍照時，則是 pictures time。如果是「拍自拍」，英文是 take a selfie；「拍團體照」則是 take a groupie。

• 關於「拍照的經典台詞」，你還能這樣說：

Shall we take a selfie?
我們來拍張自拍吧！

Let's take a groupie.
我們來拍張團體照。

On the count of three. One, two, three, cheese!
數到三，一、二、三，西瓜甜不甜？

shall　應該	selfie　自拍	groupie　團體照

2. Could you take a picture for me? 你可以幫我拍張照嗎？

> take a picture 拍照

旅遊時經常需要請別人幫忙拍照，因此，這句超好用的問句一定要學起來：
Could you take a picture ／ photo for me? 本句中的 for 表示「為了」，而 take
a picture for me 也就是「幫我拍張照」的意思。另外，take a picture of me 的
意思則是「為我拍照」，表示照片中的主角是「我」；而 take a picture with...
則是「與……拍照」。這幾句意思的差異都來自介系詞的不同。

有時，熱心幫忙拍照的路人自己也想拍張照，他們可能會問：Can you take
mine too?「你可以也幫我拍嗎？」或是我們自己可以主動說：I can take yours
later.「我待會兒也可以幫你拍。」拍完後，我們可以說：That looks great.
Thank you for your help.「真好看，謝謝你的幫忙。」

• 關於「請別人幫忙拍照」，你還能這樣說：

Sorry to bother you, but can you take my picture please?
不好意思，打擾一下，你可以幫我拍張照嗎？

Can you take a picture of me with the bridge?
你可以幫我跟這座橋拍張照嗎？

Can I take a picture with you?
我可以和你拍張照嗎？

bother 打擾	**bridge** 橋

3. Could you get the whole tower in the background?
你可以把整座塔都拍進背景裡嗎？

> whole 整個／ tower 塔／ background 背景

在這個人人都是網紅網美的時代，大家都活在虛擬的影像裡，因此，能拍出一流
的「照騙」似乎比化妝打扮的功夫更重要了。即使出門在外請路人拍照，也不能
放過任何一個角度和細節啊！本句 get...in the background 意思是「把……拍進
背景」，而「近景」的英文則是 foreground。如果最後你對別人幫你拍的照片不

滿意，你可以禮貌地説：Can you take another one, please?「你可以再幫我拍一張嗎？」

> [註]：各種鏡頭術語的英文：low-angle shot 仰角鏡頭／ high-angle shot 俯角鏡頭／ wide-angle shot 廣角鏡頭／ close-up shot 特寫鏡頭／ vertical shot (composition) 垂直構圖／ horizontal shot (composition) 水平構圖

- 關於「拍照要求」，你還能這樣說：

I'd like a full-body shot.
我要全身照。

Just my upper body.
照上半身就好。

Can you try shooting against the sun?
你可以試試背光拍攝嗎？

full-body 全身的	shot 照相	upper 上半部的
shoot 拍攝	against 正對著	

4. Can you get closer together?　你們可以靠近一點嗎？

> close 靠近的

旅行時，我們經常需要路人攝影師的幫忙，同樣地，我們也很可能成為路人的攝影師，因此，攝影師常用到的幾句英文我們也可以背起來。

- 關於「攝影師拍照指示」，你還能這樣說：

Can you take one step closer to me?
你可以向前一步嗎？

Can you go back one step?
你可以往後一步嗎？

Turn your face a little bit to the right.
臉往右邊側一點。

take one step closer 靠近一步

5. How do I do this flash thing?　這個閃光燈怎麼用？

flash　閃光燈

使用別人的相機或手機拍照時，經常會遇到不會操作的情況，比如：不會設定閃光燈時，我們可以問：How do I do this flash thing?「這個閃光燈怎麼用？」在本句中我們可以看到：美國人很喜歡用 ...thing 來表達一個模糊的分類概念，如：It's a language thing.「這是語言方面的問題。」；It's a girl thing.「這是女孩子的事情。」；It's a cultural thing.「這是文化方面的事情。」等。

• 關於「相機怎麼操作」，你還能這樣說：

You just press the button on the top of the camera.
你只要按下相機上的這個按鈕就行。

I think I pressed the wrong button.
我好像按錯了。

I think you've run out of memory.
你應該是記憶體用完了。

| press 按 | button 按鈕 | top 頂部 |
| run out of 用完 | memory 記憶體 | |

6. This photo flatters you.　你在這張照片裡比你本人好看。

flatter　過分誇讚

flatter 這個字常常和 photo「照片」一起搭配出現。比如：flattering photo 就是我們常說的「照騙」，也就是照片比本人好看，或是說：The photo flatters you.「你在這張照片裡比你本人好看。」如果是「本人比照片好看」則是：The photo doesn't flatter you. 其他描述照片的英文還有：too bright「太亮」、too dark「太暗」、overexposed「曝光過度」、out of focus「沒有對焦」、blurry「模糊的」。

• 關於「描述照片」，你還能這樣說：

I'm not photogenic.
我很不上鏡。

Your face filled up the entire frame.
你的臉佔滿了整張照片。

You cut me out of the picture.
你把我切掉了。

photogenic 上鏡的	fill up 佔滿	entire 全部的
frame 框	cut off 裁掉	

7. I'm gonna put it on Instagram. 我要放在 Instagram 上。

put on 放到……上

凹完造型擺拍後，就是將照片 po 上各種社群平台的時間了。我們一般說的 po 也就是 post「張貼」，或是 put on...「放上……」口語也很常見。接下來，我們繼續來學學「標記」、「濾鏡」和「P 圖」的英文吧！

- 關於「分享照片」，你還能這樣說：

Can I tag you in the photo?
我這張照片可以標記你嗎？

Did you add a filter to it?
你有加濾鏡嗎？

Please Photoshop it before you put it on Facebook.
上傳臉書前請先修一下圖。

tag 標記	filter 濾鏡	Photoshop 修圖
Facebook 臉書		

8. What camera did you use?　你是用什麼相機拍的？

camera　相機

如果你是攝影內行，和別人聊起攝影時，一堆器材的英文卻說不出口，那肯定鬱悶極了！這裡幾個單字和句型學起來，讓你不會因為破英文而有損帥氣的專業形象。

> [註]：各種相機器材的英文：DSLR (Digital Single-Lens Reflex) 數位單眼／ mirrorless camera 微單眼／ point and shoot camera 隨拍相機／ camera body 機身／ lens 鏡頭／ prime lens 定焦鏡頭／ zoom lens 變焦鏡頭／ wide-angle lens 廣角鏡頭／ fisheye lens 魚眼鏡頭／ shutter 快門／ flip-out screen 翻轉式螢幕／ dial 模式轉盤／ lens cover 鏡頭蓋／ lens hood 遮光罩

• 關於「拍照器材」，你還能這樣說：

I took it on my Canon D700.
我用佳能 D700 拍的。

It specializes in video.
它主打拍影片。

It takes good portraits.
這台用來拍人像很好。

specialize 專精於	portrait 人像

9. Look at this photo of my son.　看看我兒子的這張照片。

photo　照片

這個時代，誰不會趁上班空檔、茶餘飯後的時間在社群平台上刷照片、互相分享呢！？不想跟你的朋友脫節，那至少要學上幾句刷照片時用的會話吧！

• 關於「看照片說故事」，你還能這樣說：

Where was it taken?
這張在哪裡拍的？

Who took that?

這張是誰拍的？

Who is that in the photo?

照片裡的那位是誰？

---

take 拍照

---

10. Are you into photography?　你喜歡攝影嗎？

> photography　攝影

最後，我們來學學和別人聊攝影時常用的句子。「攝影」這門學問叫 photography。「喜歡攝影」我們可以用上先前學過的 into 這個字：I'm into photography. 意思便是「我很喜歡攝影。」如果是「攝影狂」或「攝影魔人」，我們則可以說：photophile。

- 關於「攝影愛好」，你還能這樣說：

She is a total photophile.

她是個攝影狂。

It's all about the light.

光線決定一切。

What camera setting did you use?

你用什麼模式拍攝的？

---

total 完全的	**photophile** 攝影癡迷者	**light** 光線
setting 設置		

1. shutterbug　攝影狂

哈哈：Jack has spent over a million dollars on her cameras. So crazy.
傑克已經花了超過一百萬元在她的相機上了，超誇張的！

Lyla：He's been known as a shutterbug.
大家都知道他是個攝影狂。

2. Uncle Bob　擁有昂貴的攝影器材，但技術水平極低並愛吹噓的攝影師

哈哈：Oh, no! Uncle Bob's coming! We'd better stay away from him.
喔不！攝影魔人來了！我們最好遠離他。

Lyla：Do you see your camera in your hands? Hide it!
看到你手上的相機了嗎？快藏起來啊！

3. photobomb　亂入照片

哈哈：Come check this picture out! You look so funny in it.
快來看這張照片！妳看起來好好笑喔！

Lyla：Tell me about it. And you photobombed it!
別說了！而且你還亂入！

4. picture-perfect　完美無瑕的

哈哈：How did your presentation go this morning?
妳今天早上的報告怎麼樣？

Lyla：It went amazingly well. Everything was picture-perfect.
非常好，一切都太完美了。

5. out of the picture　不在場的；離開的

哈哈：What happened to Cindy? She used to hang out quite a lot with you, but recently she seems to have drifted out of the picture.
Cindy 怎麼了？她之前常常和妳們一起玩，但是最近好像都不太出現了。

Lyla：Well, it's a long story. But in a word, she just doesn't get along with us.
嗯……說來話長，但簡單說，她和我們處不太來。

第 24 章 哈啦開車

角色：哈哈（來自台灣）、Lyla（來自美國）

開車之於某些人，也許是個嗜好，但對於新手來說，可能是非常令人神經緊繃的。開車上路會遇到的狀況豈止千百種，而這些狀況用英文又該怎麼表達呢？本章節我們就來聊聊開車族都會用上的十類開車英文。

1. Shotgun!　我要坐前座！

> shotgun　副駕駛座

shotgun 是一個美國的俚語，原本的意思是「獵槍」，後來被用來代指「汽車的副駕駛座」。原因是從前的美國西部，當馬車行經危險的區域時，副駕駛座常需要一位配有獵槍的保鑣來保護駕駛人的安全。因此，「坐副駕駛座」我們可以說：take the shotgun seat。另外，叫別人「上車」，我們可以說 get in the car，更口語的說法則是 hop in。

• 關於「開車常用語錄」，你還能這樣說：

Buckle up!
繫好安全帶！

Eyes on the road.
眼睛看路。

Look out!
小心！

> buckle　扣

2. I am just pulling onto the highway.　我剛上高速公路。

> pull onto　開上／ highway　高速公路

開車的時候，如何及時地表達自己的行車方向呢？如果我們要說：「開進……」，我們可以說：pull into...，如：I'm just pulling into the parking lot.「我剛開進停車場。」；「開上……」是 pull onto...，「開下」則是 get off。而「左轉」、「右轉」除了 turn left、turn right 之外，還可以說：make a left、make a right。「迴轉」則是 turn around、U-turn 或 make a U-turn。

- 關於「行車方向」，你還能這樣說：

I missed my turn.
我錯過轉彎的地方了。

You are gonna veer off to the right.
你等等要往右側行駛。

I think you're going the wrong way.
我覺得你走錯路了。

miss 錯過	turn 轉彎	veer 轉向

3. How was the drive?　開過來一路都還好嗎？

> drive 行車

朋友剛開車到自己家作客，我們可以問一句：How was the drive?「開過來一路都還好嗎？」來關切一下路上的車況如何。如果車況一切順暢，我們可以說：It was smooth.「一切順暢。」；如果車況擁堵，我們可以說：We got tied up in traffic.「我們被困在車陣中。」traffic 這個字的意思就是「交通流量」，因此，a lot of traffic 和 heavy traffic 都可以指「交通擁堵」，如：There was a lot of traffic on the 78.「78 號公路塞車很嚴重。」、I was late to the meeting due to heavy traffic.「我因為塞車開會遲到了。」

- 關於「路況」，你還能這樣說：

I got stuck in traffic near Redding.
我在 Redding 附近遇上塞車了。

The traffic is crazy. We're moving at a snail's pace.
塞車超嚴重的，我們正龜速行駛中。

It's always a nightmare to drive in the city center.
在市中心開車是個永遠的惡夢。

stuck 困住的	traffic 交通堵塞	snail 蝸牛
pace 步調	nightmare 惡夢	city center 市中心

4. I got pulled over by the police.　我被警察攔下來了。

> pull over　使靠邊停車／police　警察

在很多電影裡，尤其是警匪追逐的場景，警察會在警車內用擴音器對著在公路上疾速飛奔的歹徒大喊：Pull over!「靠邊停車！」而這句 pull over 相信大家都耳熟能詳了！在美國開車也一定得聽得懂這句 pull over，並且乖乖照做喔！很多時候其實只是一個 routine spot check「例行定點檢查」，如果自己沒有違規、違法，完全可以大方受檢。千萬不要跟美國的警察胡攪蠻纏或輕浮地開玩笑，否則惹上更大的麻煩更加得不償失。其他像是「下車」step out of the vehicle、「雙手搭在方向盤上」put your hands on the steering wheel、「我可以看一下你的駕照嗎？」May I see your driver's license? 等，也都是道路檢查時常出現的句子。

- 關於「開車違規」，你還能這樣說：

You just ran a red light.
你剛剛闖紅燈了。

You were going twenty miles over the speed limit.
你剛剛超速二十英里了。

I got a speeding ticket.
我拿到一張超速罰單。

run a red light　闖紅燈	mile　英里	speed limit　速限
speeding ticket　超速罰單		

5. The black car just cut me off.　那部黑車超我車。

> cut off　超車

不管在哪裡開車，多多少少都會遇上所謂的「馬路三寶」，也就是不文明行車的駕駛，這時候心裡總會想咒罵幾句。在我們出口成髒之前，我們先一起來學學幾個描述三寶行徑的英文吧！「超車」我們可以說 cut me off 或 overtake me；「闖紅燈」可以是 run the red light 或 jump the lights；「霸佔車道」是 hog the lane；「急停煞車」是 last-minute braking；「飆車」則是 speeding。

- 關於「不文明行車」，你還能這樣說：

The Lexus behind us is tailgating us.
我們後面那台雷克薩斯一直近距離跟車。

The red car just came out of nowhere.
那部紅車突然竄出來。

Use your turn signal!
打方向燈可以嗎！

tailgate 近距離跟車	out of nowhere 不知從哪	turning signal 方向燈

6. Fill it up, please. 加滿，謝謝。

> fill up 填滿

美國大部分的加油站都是自助加油，但當遇上人工加油的機會時，這些句子便可派上用場。「加油」的英文是 fuel up，如：I need to fuel up before getting on the highway.「我上高速公路之前需要先加個油。」；而「加滿」叫做 fill it up 或 full tank，也可以說：top it off。如果要說「加……錢的……油」，則可以說：I need...dollars of..., please.

- 關於「加油」，你還能這樣說：

My tank is almost empty.
我的車快沒油了。

I'd like forty dollars of regular, please.
我要加四十元的普通汽油，謝謝。

Can you check the tires, please?
你可以幫我檢查一下輪胎嗎？

tank 油箱 tire 輪胎	empty 空的	regular 普通汽油

7. Something is making a noise. 有個東西一直在發出怪聲。

> noise 噪音

車子最常遇到的問題就是發出怪聲，這句「什麼東西一直在發出怪聲啊？」我們可以說：What's that sound? Something is making a noise. 或 It makes a strange noise. 值得一學的是，在描述類似的問題時，我們常可以使用現在進行式或未來簡單式。比如：The windshield wipers aren't working.「雨刷壞掉了。」用的是現在進行式，而 The rear view mirror won't stay up.「後照鏡一直鬆脫掉下來。」則是用未來簡單式。

• 關於「車子出現問題」，你還能這樣說：

It keeps stalling.
車子一直熄火。

The engine won't start.
引擎發不動。

My car engine is acting up again.
我汽車的引擎又壞掉了。

stall 熄火	engine 引擎	start 啟動
act up 故障		

8. My car just broke down. Can you send someone to help?
我的車故障了，你可以派人來幫我嗎？

> break down 故障／send 派送

當不幸遇到車子半路拋錨時，一定要學會打道路救援（roadside assistance）專線，這時，這幾個簡單的句子就成了救命金句啦！除了告訴救援人員發生的問題之外，具體地表述自己的位置也非常重要，比如：I'm in the northbound lane of the 53, about 20 miles from the East Los Angeles Interchange.「我在北向 53 號公路上，距離東洛杉磯交流道大約二十英里。」或指出一個 nearest landmark「最近的地標」。總之，保持冷靜，用最簡單有效的句子來表述自己的問題，才能在最短的時間內把問題解決。

- 關於「車子故障」，你還能這樣說：

I got a flat.
我的輪胎爆胎了。

Do you have a spare part?
你有備用零件嗎？

What's the estimated cost of repairs?
維修的費用大概多少錢？

flat 爆胎	spare part 備用零件	estimated 預估的
cost 費用	repair 修理	

9. We just had a fender-bender.　我們出了點小事故。

fender-bender 輕微交通事故

說到「車禍」，我們通常是用 car accident，比較嚴重的會說 car crash，而如果是相對輕微的擦撞或追尾，我們會用 fender-bender 這個字，搭配的句型是 had a fender-bender。不管是多嚴重的車禍，記得最正確的作法一定是 call the police「報警」。

- 關於「交通事故」，你還能這樣說：

We had a minor accident.
我們發生了一點小事故。

Can somebody call 911?
有人可以幫忙打 911 嗎？

I've got insurance.
我有保險。

minor 輕微的	accident 意外	insurance 保險

10. I have a terrible sense of direction.　我的方向感很差。

> terrible　極差的／ sense of directions　方向感

開車時最怕遇到「路癡」了。在英文裡沒有剛好對應「路癡」的單字，但我們可以說：have a terrible sense of directions 或 be poor with directions 來表示某人方向感極差。路癡可能是天生的，但是我們不能當「啞巴」，方向感不好，那就多練練口語，開口問路吧！

- 關於「開車的難點」，你還能這樣說：

I'm bad with directions.
我的方向感很差。

I get lost a lot.
我很常迷路。

I always struggle with driving in reverse.
我很不會倒車。

get lost　迷路	struggle with 有……的困難	reverse　倒車

 跟開車有關的慣用語

1. backseat driver　張嘴司機（喜歡指揮司機的乘客）

哈哈：You should driver more slowly. Now you're too slow. Can you drive faster?
妳應該開慢點。現在妳又太慢了，可以開快一點嗎？

Lyla：Shut up, backseat driver!
閉嘴！別只會出一張嘴！

2. Sunday driver　開車極慢的人

哈哈：What took you so long to get here?
妳怎麼那麼晚才到？

Lyla：Sorry. I got stuck behind some Sunday driver on the road.

抱歉，我在路上被一個開車超慢的人堵了好久。

3. a lead foot　喜歡開快車的人

哈哈：You're such a lead foot when it comes to driving.

妳真的很喜歡開快車欸！

Lyla：I admit, so I've got my fair share of speeding tickets.

我承認，所以我收到的罰單也不少。

4. be in the driving seat　掌控局面

哈哈：How did the negotiation go?

談判談得怎麼樣？

Lyla：Not bad. I felt I was in the driving seat.

還不錯，我覺得我掌控了局面。

5. behind the wheel　開車

哈哈：Can you not drive like a lunatic?

妳可以不要開起車來像瘋子一樣嗎？

Lyla：No, I can't. I am indeed a different person when I'm behind the wheel.

沒辦法，我開起車來的確會變一個人。

第 25 章　哈啦上廁所

角色：哈哈（來自台灣）、Lyla（來自美國）

大千世界，連上廁所也可以上出文化差異。從讓歐美人摔得四腳朝天的亞洲蹲，到讓亞洲人大發怨言的歐洲付費廁所，從此就能體現出即使是最原始的生理呼喚，也會產生大相逕庭的習慣。不過，關於上廁所，我們還是能和外國人聊出許多有趣的共通點。現在，我們就一起來學學也許是整本書中最有味道的廁所英文吧！

1. Where is the bathroom? 請問洗手間在哪？

> **bathroom** 洗手間

出門在外必定會需要用上的問句：Where is the bathroom?「請問洗手間在哪？」其中，廁所還可以說：restroom、washroom、toilet、lavatory、loo、john 等。其中，lavatory 一般是指「飛機上的廁所」，而 loo 是英式說法、john 是美式說法。如果是在別人家作客需要借用洗手間，則是：Can I use your bathroom?「我可以借用你的洗手間嗎？」

- 關於「洗手間在哪」，你還能這樣說：

Where can I find the restroom?
請問洗手間在哪？

Can you tell me where the toilet is?
你可以告訴我洗手間在哪嗎？

Which way is the washroom?
請問洗手間在哪？

restroom 洗手間	**toilet** 廁所	**washroom** 洗手間

2. I need to take a leak. 我要小便。

> take a leak 小便

「小便」比較正式的說法是 urinate；比較口語的說法有：answer nature's call、take a leak、take a pee、take a piss、go pee、take a number 1；比較童趣的說法則是 twinkle。

- 關於「小便」，你還能這樣說：

I am going number 1.
我要去小便。

My son peed on himself again.
我兒子又尿褲子了。

I nearly wet my pants.
我差點尿褲子。

number 1 小便	pee on oneself 尿褲子	nearly 差點
wet one's pants 尿褲子		

3. I need to go take a dump first. 我要先去上大號。

> take a dump 上大號

「大號」也有好幾種說法，比較正式的是 defecate；口語一點的可以說：take a dump、take a crap、take a poop、poo、take a number 2、have a bowel movement 等。

- 關於「大號」，你還能這樣說：

The baby just pooed her pants.
這個嬰兒剛大號在褲子上了。

How often do you have a bowel movement?
你多久上一次大號？

I need to take a number 2.
我要去上大號。

| poo 上大號 | pants 褲子 | bowel movement 大號 |
| number 2 大號 | | |

4. My bladder is gonna explode.　我的膀胱快爆了。

bladder 膀胱／explode 爆炸

人生中最難受的事莫過於內急時四下遍尋不著廁所，這時別人如果問你怎麼了，你便可以説：I need to use the bathroom.「我想上廁所。」、Where's the nearest toilet?「最近的廁所在哪？」，詼諧一點時可以説：My bladder is gonna explode.「我的膀胱快爆了。」

• 關於「憋尿」，你還能這樣說：

Can you hold it? We're almost there.
你忍得了嗎？我們快到了。

Are you gonna be long? I can't hold it.
你要很久嗎？我快忍不住了。

I'm sorry, but I REALLY need to use the bathroom.
不好意思，我真的需要上洗手間。

| hold 忍 | long 久 |

5. I had the runs this morning and nearly lost my life.

我今天早上拉肚子拉到快死了。

肚子痛、拉肚子最難受了，不管是就醫或跟朋友求助，我們都需要知道相關的英文句子。其中，「腹痛」的英文是 abdominal pain、have a stomachache 或 have an upset stomach；「拉肚子」醫學的説法是 have diarrhea，比較生活化的則是 have the runs，可以想像 runs 就是「跑廁所」的意思。

• 關於「拉肚子」，你還能這樣説：

I had diarrhea.
我拉肚子了。

I'm having a stomachache.
我肚子痛。

My stomach is killing me.
我的胃快痛死了。

diarrhea 腹瀉	stomachache 肚子痛	stomach 胃
kill 殺		

6. I get diarrhea when I feel anxious. 我焦慮的時候都會拉肚子。

有人天生鐵胃，百毒不侵，有人則是一吃到辣或不新鮮的東西便會馬上肚痛拉肚子。在英文中，「鐵胃」我們可以説：have a strong stomach，而「敏感型腸胃」則是 sensitive stomach。也有一種人是所有情緒都會反應到腸胃上，如這句：I get diarrhea when I feel anxious.「我焦慮的時候都會拉肚子。」除此之外，讓我們繼續來看看還有什麼類型的腸胃吧！

• 關於「消化系統」，你還能這樣説：

I have a strong stomach. I can eat anything without getting ill.
我有個鐵胃，吃什麼東西都不會不舒服。

I have a low tolerance for spicy food.
我很不能吃辣。

I've been having constipation for weeks.
我便秘好幾週了。

ill 生病的	low 低的	tolerance 容忍度
spicy 辣的	constipation 便秘	

7. Please keep the bathroom clean. 請保持洗手間整潔。

> keep 保持／clean 乾淨的

聊完了腸胃、大小便，現在我們換聊「廁所」吧！上公共廁所或有人來自家借用廁所時，我們可能會跟他們說到各種廁所整潔的要求。其中，「保持洗手間整潔」便是 keep the bathroom clean 或 keep clean the bathroom。而「沖水」的英文則是 flush，「把⋯⋯沖進廁所」可以說：flush...down the toilet。

• 關於「廁所整潔」，你還能這樣說：

Please flush the toilet after use.
使用完畢請沖水。

Please clean up after yourself.
使用完畢後請清潔乾淨。

Please don't flush toilet tissue down the toilet.
請勿將廁紙丟進馬桶裡。

flush 沖水	toilet 馬桶	use 使用
tissue 衛生紙		

8. This restroom is not in use.　這間洗手間不開放使用。

restroom　洗手間

在外如廁時，時不時會遇到廁所清潔中或暫停使用的情況，我們可能會聽到別人說：This restroom is not in use. 或 This restroom is out of service.「這間洗手間不開放使用。」而關於廁所門把上的標示，如果是「使用中」，通常會顯示 occupied，而「可使用」則是 vacant。

• 關於「廁所不能用」，你還能這樣說：

Someone's in there.
有人在用。

Is it occupied?
廁所有人嗎？

The toilet is closed for cleaning.
這間洗手間正清潔中不開放使用。

occupied　被佔用的

9. You don't want to use that toilet.　你不會想要上那間廁所的。

toilet　廁所

不知道你是不是也很怕在外上廁所呢？即使是乾淨的廁所，上起來也難免會不自在，更何況又髒又臭的公廁呢！比起置身污穢的廁所，那忍個一兩個鐘頭可能也算不了什麼了吧！形容廁所「噁心」、「髒亂」，我們可以用 nasty 和 disgusting 這兩個形容詞，如：The toilet is nasty. You don't want to use it.「那間廁所好髒，你不會想要用的。」值得一提的是：You don't want to... 是一個滿常用的「為別人預設立場」的句型，通常用來表示「某事對於對方來說不是一件好事」的情況，如：You don't want to know what she said.「你不會想知道她說了什麼的。」

• 關於「廁所髒亂」，你還能這樣說：

The toilet really grossed me out.
那間廁所真的超噁心的。

I never use public toilets.
我從來不上公共廁所。

Did you stink up my bathroom?
你把我的廁所弄臭了嗎？

gross…out 使……感到噁心	public toilet 公共廁所	stink 使……變臭

10. The toilet seems to be clogged.　馬桶好像堵住了。

seem 似乎／ clog 堵塞

最後，我們來聊聊各種關於廁所的神奇現象。舉凡馬桶不通、女廁永遠大排長龍、關鍵時候廁紙用完、烘手機大半天烘不乾手等。看看是不是也讓你心有戚戚焉呢？

• 關於「廁所大小事」，你還能這樣說：

There's a huge line for the girls' restroom.
女廁排隊的人超多的。

I have run out of toilet paper.
我的廁紙用完了。

It takes forever for the hand dryer to dry my hands.
等烘手機烘乾我的手我都八十歲了。

restroom 洗手間	run out of 用完	toilet paper 廁紙
hand dryer 烘手機	dry 烘乾	

1. relieve oneself　上廁所

Lyla：We need to get going. The train leaves at four thirty.
我們得走了，火車四點半發車。

哈哈：Hold on a second. I need to go relieve myself.
等一下，我要先去上個廁所。

2. spend a penny　上廁所

哈哈：How long is the bus ride?
巴士要坐多久啊？

Lyla：It's three and a half hours, so you'd better go spend a penny
before you leave.
三個半小時，所以出發前你最好先去上個廁所。

3. go down the toilet　走下坡；揮霍殆盡

哈哈：The actor's reputation has gone down the toilet since he made
a racist comment on his Facebook.
自從上次在臉書上發表種族歧視的言論後，這位男演員的名聲已一
敗塗地了。

Lyla：Well…he has to pay for what he said.
嗯……他得為自己說過的話付出代價啊！

4. potty mouth　髒話連篇的人

哈哈：I've had enough of Dora. She never stops swearing.
我受夠 Dora 了，她一直講髒話。

Lyla：She has a potty mouth. I don't like her either.
她很愛講髒話，我也不喜歡她。

5. piss off　惹生氣

哈哈：You think Mr. Yang will be pissed off if I'm late.
　　　妳覺得如果我遲到的話楊老師會生氣嗎？

Lyla：I think he's already pissed off. You'd better hurry.
　　　我想他已經生氣了，你最好快點。

語研力 E088

用趣味漫畫學生活英語：
跟老外聊天輕鬆開話題

作　　者　徐培恩（Ryan）◎著
顧　　問　曾文旭
出版總監　陳逸祺、耿文國
主　　編　陳蕙芳
繪　　者　徐培恩（Ryan）
美術編輯　李依靜
法律顧問　北辰著作權事務所

印　　製　世和印製企業有限公司
初　　版　2023年10月
(本書為《哈啦英文1000句：「圖像導引法」，帶你破冰、不尬聊，自信、舒適、流暢地用英語閒聊生活樂事（隨掃即聽「哈啦英語」QR Code）》之修訂版)
出　　版　凱信企業集團－凱信企業管理顧問有限公司
電　　話　（02）2773-6566
傳　　真　（02）2778-1033
地　　址　106 台北市大安區忠孝東路四段218之4號12樓
信　　箱　kaihsinbooks@gmail.com

定　　價　新台幣349元／港幣116元
產品內容　1 書

總 經 銷　采舍國際有限公司
地　　址　235 新北市中和區中山路二段366巷10號3樓
電　　話　（02）8245-8786
傳　　真　（02）8245-8718

國家圖書館出版品預行編目資料

用趣味漫畫學生活英語：跟老外聊天輕鬆開話
題／徐培恩著. -- 初版. -- 臺北市：凱信企業集
團凱信企業管理顧問有限公司, 2023.10
　面；　公分
ISBN 978-626-7354-05-6(平裝)

1.CST: 英語 2.CST: 會話 3.CST: 漫畫

805.188　　　　　　　　　　112014233

凱信企管

用對的方法充實自己，
讓人生變得更美好！

凱信企管

用對的方法充實自己，
讓人生變得更美好！